D1411900

WEB LARGE PRINT
Webster, Ja   24-
One little

AUG 31 1988

WEB LARGE PRINT
Webster, Jan, 1924-
One little room

AUG 31 1988

DATE	ISSUED TO
SEP. 1 5 1988	Mary Smith
OCT. 1 — 1988	Gussie Burns

Webster

One li

SEP. 1 5 1988

OCT. 1 — 19

CONN. STATE LIBRARY
LIBRARY SERVICE CENTER
WILLIMANTIC, CONN.

AUG 31 1988

SPECIAL MESSAGE TO READERS

This book is published by
THE ULVERSCROFT FOUNDATION,
a registered charity in the U.K., No. 264873

The Foundation was established in 1974 to provide funds to help towards research, diagnosis and treatment of eye diseases. Below are a few examples of contributions made by THE ULVERSCROFT FOUNDATION:

★ A new Children's Assessment Unit
  at Moorfield's Hospital, London.

★ Twin operating theatres at the
  Western Ophthalmic Hospital, London.

★ The Frederick Thorpe Ulverscroft Chair of
  Ophthalmology at the University of Leicester.

★ Eye Laser equipment to various eye hospitals.

If you would like to help further the work of the Foundation by making a donation or leaving a legacy, every contribution, no matter how small, is received with gratitude. Please write for details to:

THE ULVERSCROFT FOUNDATION,
**The Green, Bradgate Road, Anstey,
Leicestershire, LE7 7FU. England.**
Telephone: (0533) 364325

ONE LITTLE ROOM

Brought up in straitened circumstances, sisters Catherine and Christie-Ann fall in love with the same man. Catherine turns him down fearful above all things of remaining poor, and instead marries an Army officer. Christie-Ann first comforts then marries the rejected suitor. But the secret bond between the two sisters looks set to destroy both marriages and bring suffering on all four protagonists. This story of conflicting needs begins in a bleak wartime Scotland and continues through more prosperous post-war years.

JAN WEBSTER

ONE LITTLE ROOM

Complete and Unabridged

CONNECTICUT STATE LIBRARY
LIBRARY DEVELOPMENT DIVISION
LIBRARY SERVICE CENTER
WILLIMANTIC, CONNECTICUT

ULVERSCROFT
Leicester

WEB
LARGE
PRINT

First published in Great Britain in 1987 by
Robert Hale Ltd.,
London

First Large Print Edition
published May 1988
by arrangement with
Robert Hale Ltd.,
London

Copyright © 1987 by Jan Webster
All rights reserved

British Library CIP Data

Webster, Jan
  One little room.—Large print ed.—
Ulverscroft large print series: general fiction
I. Title
823'.914[F]   PR6073.E2313

  ISBN 0-7089-1809-3

Published by
F. A. Thorpe (Publishing) Ltd.
Anstey, Leicestershire
Set by Rowland Phototypesetting Ltd.
Bury St. Edmunds, Suffolk
Printed and bound in Great Britain by
T. J. Press (Padstow) Ltd., Padstow, Cornwall

"For love, all love of other sights
   controls,
And makes one little room, an
   everywhere."

John Donne

"*Angels guard me at my bed,
One at the foot and one at the head.*"
Oh, those angels!
"Ma-ammie!"
"I'll come in there and leather you if you're not quiet."
Door shut. No crack. Not the faintest.
Dark and the angels.
Come in, Mammie. Speak to me. I won't cry any more. I won't call out. I promise. Lay your hand on me. Tuck me in. Kiss me on the forehead. You never kiss me. You don't even like me. You like Christie-Ann the best. Christie-Ann sleeps with you. The wind is coming down the chimney to get me. I'll be good, Mammie. I'll be good.

I promise.

1

SNOW speckled the bare, chaste streets. Shopkeepers had nothing to display in their windows, save dummy packets or tins, or notices which proclaimed "No Oranges", "No Matches", "Do not ask for extra as a refusal often offends".

The windows were in any case criss-crossed with brown tape against bomb blast. Sandbags and baffle walls stood at the mouths of tenements.

Everything looked bare, minimal, grudging of human comfort. But then Dounhead had always been a place denied. Maybe it was just a little barer, a little colder, a little bleaker that day, than it had ever been. They came out of the church and stood, like figures in a weather-vane, on the chilly, frosty steps, just two of the hastily-married in the Year of Our Lord, 1941.

"She's a hard little madam," said one wedding onlooker, who had tied her pallid face and greasy hair up in a wrinkled head-scarf against the biting cold.

"Aye. Close, too. You can never tell what's going on behind that touch-me-not expression of hers," averred her friend in the shambling fur-lined boots. "But she's been the breadwinner, she's that clever at the shorthand and typing. What's Lizzie Bathgate going to do now?"

They looked at each other and laughed without generosity. The hope was that Lizzie Bathgate would sink rather than swim. Her, with her conviction that she was a cut above everybody else and her two daughters who were always tidier, smarter, sharper than the rest. There was no doubt that Catherine, the elder, had made a catch—an English Army captain, no less. There he was, looking like an elegant greyhound among so many shaggy Lowland Scottish mongrels, on this shivering, snow-threatened wartime morning.

But though the bride moved palely, smilingly, bandbox glamorous behind her hat's pink veiling, the women did not miss the look of anxiety pulling at Lizzie's mouth. They never missed things like that in Dounhead. Lizzie Bathgate must feel the ground shifting under her feet. Not just her financial security threatened, but her position as family *Gauleiter*. A married daughter could not be managed, kept in her place, like an unmarried one. The women, however, withheld their sympathy. It would teach her she was no better than anybody else, a lesson badly needed. Dounhead believed in such lessons.

Lizzie Bathgate had perhaps forgotten about her drunken old father and the days when she had been pauper-poor. A little shake-up was just what she needed.

Wrinkled Headscarf, however, dissembled with practised skill as Catherine Bathgate and her groom Edward Elkins emerged from the grey and mahogany shadows of Dounhead Parish Church. Laying her hand on the girl's arm, she said with a show of concern, "Aye, your mammie'll miss you, hen."

"Scarcely," said Catherine Bathgate sweetly. "I'll still be living with her, you know, Mrs. Macfarlane. While Edward is away. While the war is still on."

"Aye, but it's got to end some day."

Shambling Boots contributed a nod and a brief wait-and-see smile before chucking a meagre handful of rice on Catherine's bent head. It was difficult to tell which was snow, which rice. There is a photograph in a certain Dounhead sitting-room to this day which shows them, Catherine and Edward Elkins, as they were in their married hour. He, unbelievably callow, green, young and happy; she with those fine blue eyes hooded and the mouth trembling on the verge of—what is it?—a smile, or tears?

"What a bunch of harpies," said Edward Elkins afterwards. He wasn't being snobbish: at university he had, in fact, toyed with Socialist ideas. But Dounhead with its dispossessed women got to him, worried him. There seemed little of the gentle sex in any of them. Catherine's mother, for example, was so much tougher, more assertive and belligerent than his own gentle English one. Catherine said it was because they had to be, the men were so feeble. Years of dire unemployment had taken away their self-respect.

He was watching his wife undress with

4

the precision and despatch with which she attacked everything. What was it about the closed hauteur of that pleasantly ordinary-to-pretty face that attracted him so? The occasional vulnerability, even sadness, or the challenge to melt the ice? For two days he was determined to study his young wife in all her moods, to devote himself only to her, to forget the miserable progression of the war, the U-boats, the desolate sight of blitzed London when he'd passed through, the retreat in the desert, in Greece and in Crete. Even the pinpricks like the pathetic rationed ounce of cheese, the scrape-round for clothing coupons to provide Catherine's wedding outfit and his C.O.'s occasional flight of blistering sarcasm at his expense.

For two days Catherine was all his. Catherine, pronounced in the Scottish manner rhyming with "fine" and equal stresses on each syllable. He had fallen in love with her while watching her dance with someone else. He had never seen anyone so trim, so wonderfully in control of a lissom body. And yet there were curves, hinting at a gentle voluptuousness which had lifted Edward Elkins' mind from its customary cool and organized track into a wild, desperate wanting. He didn't need his C.O. to tell him she wasn't his class. It made no difference.

He forgot about Wrinkled Headscarf and Shambling Boots as Catherine slipped into a pink Celanese nightdress with puffed sleeves and a sweetheart neckline. He saw again how young she was: twenty to his twenty-eight. Golden hair, natural, fine yet so thick and so apparently malleable it made him think of Impressionist brush-strokes, tumbled forward and covered her face as she got into bed beside him. Oh, God, he could almost eat her clover-smelling breath . . .

The harpies' comment surfaced again the next afternoon, when they lay in each other's arms watching the Gourock rain do its best to batter in the hotel bedroom window. Innocently she had talked about being home in time to wash the kitchen out for her mother on the Friday.

"You're my wife now," he'd reminded her gently, for he was gentle in his middle-class way in everything concerning her. "When we live in London, your mother will have Christie-Ann for company. She needn't miss you that much."

"Oh, maybe we'll settle in Dounhead," said Catherine. "Somewhere near her. After all, Edward, I've never said anything about coming to England."

She could see his almost comical horror-stricken expression three times over in the triple dressing-table mirror. This was the first time Edward Elkins realized what he had done, that he had not married a blonde and malleable extension of himself (after a rash six-weeks' courtship) but someone singular, other and almost completely unknown.

But he was touched by love, in the way medieval saints he had read about were touched by God or lunacy. So it was an impasse. "Don't let's talk about it," he said as she saw him off at Glasgow Central Station when the honeymoon was over. This was to become a common strategy with him.

But she wrote to him about her feelings. "I feel part of Scotland, Edward. If I leave my mother, I shall feel like a deserter. She has had it so hard." He brooded while his battalion went on manoeuvres in the south of England and while he waited to see whether he would be sent to North Africa or be part of the Second Front in Europe.

He saw that being married meant an intermingling of wants so that in some strange way the other's desires could become yours. If she loved Scotland, then so must he. He began to see it as the romantic place of his reading, to respond to the cadences of Scott and Stevenson. Maybe they would live there, after the war. If he was not killed.

"Poor Edward," wrote his mother. *"I don't think you were ready for this. I don't think you'll mean it about living in Scotland."* But she had no power over him any more. Now his sentimental education was beginning all over again and it was Catherine alone who could teach him the language.

While he worked towards promotion to major she was called up for war work and became, as she wrote to him, "an engineer, a semi-skilled fitter, to be precise. I can weld, solder, make tools, drill, rivet, draw and read blueprints". It sounded alarming. He knew she was saving his Army allowance and teaching shorthand and typing in the evenings. She made passing references to having her own commercial college one day. When he suggested she should ease up, she wrote back "It's wonderful not to be poor any more. I've tried it and I hated it!"

She wasn't going to go where he led. She wasn't biddable, easy or the least bit like his mother in relation to his father. She wasn't going to live necessarily where he wanted to live, or wait for pearls of wisdom to fall from his lips.

It had been most uncharacteristic of him to give into his emotions like that, to want to marry her or die. It was true that the possibility of being killed had concentrated his mind wonderfully, had made him determined to know love, to taste ecstasy. Something about that wholesome, with-holding, peach-skinned face, something about her capable hands, about her calves and the way she danced, about her smell, her laugh, the way she tossed her hair . . . something about all of that had unmanned him, taken him apart, so that for a while he was only whole and functioning when she was in the same room as him. He kissed the photograph of her in her wedding hat every night before he turned out the light.

"She shouldn't have done it," said Christie-Ann Bathgate to her mother Lizzie on the night of the wedding. She had been best maid, of course, and had put away her blue bridesmaid's dress in tissue paper till it was needed for something like a Sunday School soirée or another wedding. Outside, she was aware of snow still speckling down, covering Dounhead, burying it in the gentle folds of Lowland hills.

"Well, she's married him and that's that." Lizzie's mouth clamped down over her own doubts. In the greystone cottage she finished building up the coal fire with tea leaves and potato peelings which, once they had dried out, would smoulder away and keep the coal from expending its warmth too quickly. The fire was already contracted by the use of firebricks at the side but despite all this husbanding of fuel there was talk of rationing. In an area built on coal! Rationing! Rationing! Rationing! They would ration the air next.

"She shouldn't have," said Christie-Ann again.

"Why not?" said her mother defiantly.

"You know why not. Because I think she's still in love with Colum Brodie."

"Naw, naw." Lizzie Bathgate was tired and agitated. A small, angular, positive person, she got up and twitched the blackout curtains together although she had already closed them most carefully. "You're not to mention his name again, Christie-Ann. I forbid it. Your sister is now a married woman. Married to a captain. A man with letters after his name. She is Mrs. Edward Elkins and that is how you must think of her. How could she ever have bettered herself with the likes of Colum Brodie?"

Christie-Ann sucked on a strand of her blonde-streaked brown hair. She was a darker, dumpier, softer version of Catherine, but then she was only seventeen and had not fined down all her puppy fat yet. There was something else about Christie-Ann. She never looked quite as bandbox tidy as Catherine. There was always a wayward strand of hair, a slight dishevelment about her, as though her

11

looks as well as her emotions were less capable of being kept in hand.

"I'll have him," she volunteered chirpily. "I'll have Colum Brodie, if he comes back all in one piece from the war."

Her mother gave her a look of suppressed fury. It had been a long, demanding day. She had been determined that everything would go off properly and it had, down to the last frugal sandwich and precious dish of trifle made with mock cream (cornflour, sugar and a little margarine) and the tinned fruit sent up by Edward's parents, who hadn't been able to make the journey because of the husband's recent heart attack. It had all fallen on her and she'd seen it through, but her bones felt pulverized, so weary she scarcely knew how to get them off to bed.

She put her head back on her chair and said nonetheless, like a lesson that had to be learned by her younger daughter as by her older, "The Brodies are not in our class. They're a dirty, verminous lot—"

"They're not all like the mother and father. They try quite hard. Lucille's a tidy girl. She keeps her hair nice. And Colum wanted to better himself—"

Lizzie Bathgate rose from her chair and pointed to the door.

"Get up these stairs, do you hear me? I'll no' have that man's name mentioned in this house again."

"The poor man's away fighting in the war. You can't talk about people, Mother, as though they were scum—"

The mother's small, hard hand landed with an unmerciful thud on her daughter's jaw, so that Christie-Ann's head jerked back and tears flooded into her eyes from the pain.

"What was that for?" she cried in amazement.

"It's to teach you to listen to me." Lizzie Bathgate's small frame was rigid with anger. She took Christie-Ann by the shoulders and shook her. With each shake she uttered through clenched teeth, "You'll - listen - to - me - or - I'll - knock - the - head - off - your - shoulders. Leave - the - name - of - Brodies - alone—"

The girl tussled with her mother, but she was afraid of her, too, and her efforts were defensive, not retaliatory. At length she collapsed back in her chair, holding her face and sobbing and her mother went on staggering feet into the kitchen, where she held the kettle under the tap, placed it on the gas stove to boil and came in with a damp, cold rag which she held out wordlessly to her daughter.

"Haud it to your face, or you'll have a keeker in the morning."

"So what?" demanded Christie-Ann, but doing as she was bid. "Let them see what goes on in this house. I wish I was like Catherine, married and getting out of it."

"Catherine is coming back here to live."

"Only till Edward comes home. She'll show you. And so will I. I'll get out the first chance I get. I'll get out and I'll never come back."

The mother made tea. "Get yourself a cup," she said ungraciously. The girl ignored her. Lizzie sat down and said in a low, defeated voice, "I've tried to make something of you. I've slaved and gone without since your father died, so you two could go to the Academy, have decent clothes and shoes to your feet. Who paid for Catherine's shorthand and typing classes? It was me. Cleaning, dressmaking, scraping, saving. I had to walk miles to

14

save a ha'penny on a quarter-stone of potatoes. I had to do without a new coat to my back . . . scrimp and save, that's been my life."

The girl began to weep again. "I know all that. We never asked to be born."

"I've never struck you before. But you goaded me."

"You leathered us when we were young. Catherine and me. We were terrified for the belt."

"You needed chastizing. Your father never cared. If it had been left to him you would have run wild, your clothes in tatters and your feet in parish boots. Like the Brodies."

Christie-Ann shifted uncomfortably.

"You had to be trained. Children dinna ken any better. You had to be trained to keep yourself clean and tidy, to have respect for yourselves. I had to be the one to set standards—nobody else round here does. And I've been complimented. Ladies. That's what I've reared. In spite of everything, ladies. And you—you would associate us with the likes of the Brodies. You can smell the mother before you see her. The kids were brought up to run back

15

and forth to the pawn and the whisky shop—"

"That wasn't their fault—"

"They burnt their chairs and their palings for firewood. The likes of Lucille went to school in her bare feet—"

"But when Colum and Lucille started working, it got better. You have to *admire* them for it—"

"No more." Lizzie put her cup down with a threatening rattle. "I've had enough. Brodies this. Brodies that. Your sister married someone of her own type today. She'll want for nothing from now on." She looked drained, pushed to the edge of endurance and Christie-Ann gave up her defence of the Brodies with a sigh.

"I wish I was her," said Christie-Ann feelingly. "I wish I was on my honeymoon. I wish I was a hundred miles away from here."

Christie-Ann lay broodingly in bed, listening to her mother tidy up downstairs. From the sound of it she was shifting the table and chairs to sweep the linoleum. She always behaved this way when overtired or overwrought. It was to make you feel even more guilty. Lizzie had turned

16

on the wireless and Joseph Macleod read the news, saying goodnight once, then twice, as always. When music by Harry Roy came on, her mother switched off.

Christie-Ann. The very name made her different. The intention had been to name her Ann Christie Bathgate, the middle name being her mother's surname, but the registrar had been fuddled, it having been just after New Year, and had put on the birth certificate Christie-Ann. We'll leave it, her mother said, liking the sound of it. But it had been mocked up and down school corridors from Mixed Infants to the Academy, where last year she had taken her Highers. It was part of the whole process of separating the Bathgate girls from the rest, making them different. Only recently had she begun to half-like it. At least it was better than being a Mary or a Margaret or a Jenny, or even a Catherine come to that. It was original and therefore a comfort in Christie-Ann's book.

She lay weeping softly in the dark, missing Catherine, putting a hand up from time to time to feel her face. There was a hard little bump just over the cheekbone and it might well be discoloured. She'd have to say she'd walked into a baffle wall in the blackout. People did that all the time, blacking their eyes and smashing their glasses. However angry she might be, the idea of giving her mother away was unthinkable. They were a united front and Lizzie had bred into her daughters the necessity for discretion, not telling the Dounhead gossips anything when they tried, as her mother put it, to "draw" you. "We keep ourselves to ourselves," was her mother's motto. "Nobody round here puts the bread in my mouth," she would add. "What I've got, I've worked for."

It was the truth, of course. Christie-Ann wished that adversity had not destroyed all the gaiety in her mother's nature. It was strange to think it, but the coming of the war had given them money to spare for the first time in their lives, what with Catherine's work at the armaments factory and her own job at the Food Office, working out permits for animal feed on the farms. Her mother didn't need to go out cleaning any more, but her dressmaking expertise was much sought after with clothes on coupons and people wanting this made down or that adapted or dressing-gowns fashioned from blackout material or whatever.

If only her mother could relax, but it had become a habit with her, the ranting that had grown out of exhaustion, the nagging and the bullying that had come from a white-hot determination to survive and move upwards. Christie-Ann was just old enough to remember her father's death —she had been seven and her sister ten— and the frantic borrowing that had gone on to get him buried. After that, it had been the weekly struggle to get the rent together, to get food. She suspected her mother had sometimes gone without so that she and Catherine could eat.

But she and Catherine had had a rough passage of it. They were never allowed outside the cottage to play, like other children. They played with each other. It had intensified the rivalry between them, so that often they had fought like cat and dog. Their mother had made them share the cleaning of the house, the shopping, the cooking and baking, so that at quite an early age they were proficient housekeepers. They could cut out a pattern, make their own clothes and knew to within a farthing the price of everything at the local Co-op. Their spare time was supposed to be spent knitting or reading "good books" from the small library in the Miners' Welfare, books Lizzie wiped down for germs before they read them.

It had paid off. They had done well at school, Catherine especially. Teachers had liked them for the tidy example they set. In her last two years Catherine had specialized in "commercial subjects", that was to say shorthand, typing and book-keeping and then "kept them up" at night-classes afterwards, where she'd also taken Literature. Lizzie had approved of this, especially when Catherine's proficiency in shorthand and typing brought her her teacher's certificate. "Now you'll always have something to fall back on," Lizzie had gloated and Catherine had quickly gathered up a small coterie of private pupils anxious for the skills that would reward them with work in an office rather than a shop or a factory. It also meant Catherine had a status of teacher without having been to college, another notch in Lizzie's yardstick of respectability.

But it had been at night-school she'd met Colum Brodie. Christie-Ann turned restlessly now at the thought of him, her weeping over, her face red and solemn in the dark. What was it about him? Whether her mother liked it or not, he had become a sort of lodestar in their lives. Not tall, but sort of indomitable, dark, bright, laughing, with a kind of pleading quality about him. That was right, wasn't it? A something in him that demanded to be liked, even loved. He stood out. There was only one of him. He'd always had a book under his arm and a big old scarf round his neck. She smiled at the image. Looking for an argument, be it about politics, religion, poetry. He'd started to work for the local paper, the *Dounhead Courier*, before he'd joined up. Catherine had started to help him with his shorthand.

Maybe, thought Christie-Ann, the pleading look had been to ask you not to judge him by his family. They lived, not in the humble greystone cottages or old tenements that characterized most of Dounhead, but in the Slum Clearances, new Council houses already scarred and brutalized by the poverty within them.

The father had been a pit union leader, till injured in an underground fall. From then on, he had blurred pain and misfortune in drink and wife-beating and eight little Brodies had more or less brought themselves up.

Christie-Ann thought Bridget Brodie, his mother, had once had a lovely face and Donald Brodie a bewildered intelligence showing through the degeneracy caused by drink. Privately she fantasized about the whole family, cleaning them up in her mind, trying somehow to make them "decent" or "respectable", but then some outrage like a drunken brawl between the parents in the street would send her pity and imagination scuttling for shelter. Maybe the Brodies were, as her mother said, beyond the pale.

What a pity, then, that Catherine hadn't stopped to think before meeting Colum Brodie secretly in Glasgow for the pictures and going for walks with him when her mother thought she was at night-school. It was most unlike Catherine, who had always sought above all else to please and mollify her mother.

"Oh, I love him, Christie-Ann. I've

never had a feeling like this in my life." Christie-Ann remembered her appalled excitement at her sister's words and she had never doubted their veracity. How she had wished for the same feeling to happen to her. Mixed in with her thoughts of how it had been with Catherine and Colum were her own muddied jealousies, the way she had felt all through her life when her sister got there first. Catherine had got the new clothes that would be handed down to her. Catherine had gone first to the Academy, ensuring Christie-Ann's future teachers would throw her sister's prowess in her face. Catherine got Colum first, she thought now, before drifting off to sleep, but she has no claim on him now. Why did she pick the Englishman? Was it because he'd wanted her so badly? Or was it once again to please and mollify their mother?

Lucille Brodie had stopped scuttling about like a frightened rabbit, Christie-Ann thought as she approached her. Since Colum had gone away, she had taken over the running of the family. She had had her hair permed and wore high-heeled shoes.

But there was still that half-timid, half-defensive Brodie look.

Neither girl was sure whether to stop and talk, but Christie-Ann's curiosity overcame her.

"Any word of Colum?" she asked, determinedly off-handed.

"You never heard, Christie-Ann? He's been taken prisoner in North Africa. Wounded. My mother's in an awful state."

"Badly wounded?"

"We don't know how bad. The only thing is, he might be exchanged. If it's bad enough to keep him out of the fighting in future. We've just got to wait and see."

"I'm very sorry, Lucille." The two girls, never natural protagonists, relaxed a little in each other's company.

"Are you all right for clothing coupons, Christie-Ann? With all the wee ones, we've always got one or two to spare."

"How much?"

"One-and-threepence. That's the going rate," said Lucille apologetically.

"I'll let you know," said Christie-Ann. She'd buy some, if she could think of some way of keeping it from her mother.

"Christie-Ann?" Lucille called after her.

"He's been made up to an officer. Thought you would like to know."

Christie-Ann waited till Catherine came in from the day shift at the factory and had washed the grime from her hands and face and removed her overalls and the turban covering her hair, before she relayed the news.

They were seated at the tea table and she tried to be as casual as possible about it.

"Wounded?" Catherine's protesting cry was out before she could stifle it. She half-rose from her chair, looked quickly at her mother and sat down again.

"Who told you?" That was Lizzie, gimlet-eyed.

"Lucille . . . she always talks to me—I can't stop her," said Christie-Ann quickly.

"Is it bad?" asked Catherine, spreading a piece of bread over and over with a scrape of jam.

"They don't know. They're waiting to hear."

Nothing more was said. Catherine helped Christie-Ann to clear the table and wash up before she picked up a letter that had come earlier from Edward and carried it up to her room. When Christie-Ann happened to go up to the bathroom and had to tiptoe past her sister's bedroom, she heard the sound of weeping, as she had known she would.

Catherine thought it was Fate that took her into Glasgow that day. The Central Station was clamorous, as always, with the screech and hoot of steam trains and the clanging of doors on Servicemen returning from leave.

She had noticed the ambulances draw up and then the fact that they were carrying stretcher cases from one train out to them. Her heart began to bang in her chest, so wildly she thought she would suffocate. She had just been through the shops in Sauchiehall Street, looking for something special to send Edward on his birthday, but it was Colum Brodie's name that rose to her lips and Colum Brodie's presence she sensed, even before she saw him.

"Poor laddies," said a woman, gazing through the hastily erected barriers. "I wonder where they're coming from? Looks as though their fighting days are over."

She took a packet of Capstan cigarettes from her handbag and handed them through the barrier to a young soldier half-sitting up on a stretcher, a bandage round his head and over one eye.

"Keep them, son. God bless you."

"Where are they from?" She heard herself beseeching anyone who would listen. "Are they swopped prisoners?" She groped in her own bag for sweets, precious as jewels, to hand over. She was sweating, near to tears, but her eyes raked over every casualty. And then he was there.

"Colum." She didn't know she had said his name, but his dark head turned sharply and he saw her.

"Let me . . ." she pushed onlookers aside and put her arm over the barrier. Whoever had been pushing him had gone off to see what was holding up progress towards the ambulances. He raised an arm and their hands clasped convulsively. She wasn't aware of tears coursing down her cheeks. He was so pale and pitiable, with great black streaks under his eyes, yet he held her so tightly.

"Colum," she said, "Oh, Colum, is it you?"

She was leaning over the barrier so precariously she almost toppled over and he was struggling to sit up despite one shoulder being elaborately strapped up and then their faces, their lips were touching as though nothing could keep them apart and her cheek rested on his cheek and her tears mingled with his tears.

"Clear the way." The attendant had returned. He was both shaken and amused at what was happening under his gaze.

"You'll have to wait a wee while longer for that, Missis," he said, gently. Colum was being wheeled away from her. She could see only the gleam of his smile in the sooty steam. She had given him the bar of Fry's Cream Chocolate from her handbag and he waved it now at her, with his good arm.

"Oh, Christ," she said, feeling the brief ecstasy run out of her, "what have I done? My dear love, what have I done?"

2

"DO you think you could rustle up a biscuit for us?"

"I'll see," said the very young waitress in the Bath teashop, blushing violently. She returned with two shortcake biscuits sitting forlornly in the centre of a large cracked plate.

"That's great. Thanks a lot," said Edward Elkins effusively. The little girl in her too-big apron blushed some more and Catherine could not restrain a pale smile at the tableau.

"You'd wheedle the birds out of the trees," she said to her husband.

"At least it's got a smile out of you," he answered, grimly. "Look, I don't want you to go back. But there could be another raid again tonight. It's obvious he's after historic towns now he's done his damnedest to poor old London. The Baedeker raids, that's what they're calling them in the mess. Well, if I'd known Bath

29

was for it I'd never have let you come, even if it is your holiday."

"We're supposed to be married." She gave another wan smile. "Wherever thou goest, et cetera."

"Not in wartime. I've no option but to be here. But you'll be safer in dingy old Dounhead. Even Hitler can have no interest in that."

"We've had bombs in Scotland, too," she reminded him.

Out in the pale sunshine, holding tentatively on to his arm, she had the strange sensation again of not being herself, of a kind of disembodiment. Bath looked golden and beautiful. She had not known there were places like this, places where the bing heap did not distort the landscape, where poverty, if it existed, was never obvious. She took a deep breath and shook herself out of introspection. Their sleep had been rudely punctured the night before by bombing, as savage as it had been unexpected. That no doubt accounted for the drained feeling. If she had to leave, then she wanted to take in as much as she could. Trim Street, Green Street, Gay Street, Quiet Street. Edward filled in a deft picture of the city's history in his quiet, educated voice. She felt herself carried away by the sweep of his knowledge.

Try to picture, he said, the Roman soldiers marching from London to Wales and stopping here at the garrison, footsore and weary. And then seeing the hot springs bubbling up from a fissure in the great white beds of limestone and some bright berk visualizing heated rooms, Turkish baths, swimming-pools and cubicles and alcoves where you could have a massage, drink wine or eat honey cakes. Aquae Sulis, they'd called it, dedicating it to the Celtic god Sul and their own wise healer, Minerva. She had only seen Dounhead: cold, snow-speckled. Barren.

I know nothing, she thought despairingly. *I'm a blank page. I've been nowhere, done nothing. O, my narrow, narrow life.* She trotted along obediently by Edward's side, her heels rubbing in her high-heeled best shoes, doing her best, as instructed, to think of Jane Austen's Emma coming out of this bow-fronted shop, or that other Emma, Lady

Hamilton, joining her lover Nelson on the Grand Parade.

They stopped in front of the Abbey. "Monks ruled here," he told her. "They called it Hat Batha, 'sick man's city'." She looked at the little stone figures straining up the ladders on either side, to eternity, and felt a desperate cold madness pour over her.

"Come on." Edward jolted her arm. "You'll miss your train. Don't brood about last night."

"I wasn't." She denied it. He had not been referring to the bombs, but to that other charade before the sirens went, the one going on in bed with its tears and frustration and turnings away.

She wanted to say to him, "I'm all mixed up, Edward. When you and I are together, I think of Colum. I don't want to. I want to be a proper wife to you, but something in me turns away now and won't be persuaded. And you are a nice man, Edward and have so much more to offer me than the other one. Your world of knowledge, your tolerance, your gentleness. Only he is still part of me, and you are not and how do I change that?" She could say nothing, only look at him with a silent pleading for his forbearance.

He said, with a rough surge of emotion unusual for him, "If we could forget about birth control, it would be easier for both of us."

"It was no fault of yours," she insisted quickly. "It was me. *Me!*"

"I think you're tired. The work you do is no work for a woman. My poor lovie."

She wasn't used to endearments. She thought how much she wanted kindness from him, needed it and some kind of forgiveness, too, and then they could start all over again. But she would never be able to explain. The look in his warm brown eyes made her own fill up with tears.

He took her in his arms on the station platform, oblivious to the people milling around them and kissed her long and lingeringly on the lips.

"Think about it, darling," he urged, as they drew apart. "Think about us starting a baby. If anything happened to me, you would have our child. Don't you want that? Say you want that. Please."

"Nothing is going to happen to you. The war might end soon."

"Don't you want a baby?"

"I don't know, Edward," she said miserably. He could see from her face she was not even contemplating it. But she wouldn't discuss it further. She could be maddeningly unpredictable.

He put her into her carriage and she ran the window down so that he could hold her hand. They were in a kind of numbness, so that they could say nothing. As the train started to move, he said, "I love you. I'll see you soon. Take care," and she smiled and waved and saw him dwindle with a kind of thankfulness.

One night, she and Colum had not gone to night-school but had taken a country walk instead, alongside one of Dounhead's disused pits where briar and saugh grew over the slate and clinker. It had been spring and warmth and promise had coursed through both their bodies. She had never had anyone who would listen to what she thought before. Perhaps neither had he. But it had seemed like a miracle. He was so gentle and she had never known gentleness before. He was so giving and no-one had given to her before. He had

34

held her for a long time and when he'd kissed her she'd looked over his shoulder and seen the early moon move and shudder. Later it seemed as though the stars had settled themselves in a mantle about her shoulders and the evening wind had softly combed her hair. All that had followed had been a consequence of that night. She would not take it back, even now. That kind of giving could not be undone.

The train was held up outside Swindon. A young sailor sitting next to her fell asleep and his head fell on to her shoulder. She kept easing it off but it would fall back again, a dead weight. She closed her eyes resignedly and in a troubled sleep she dreamed she was climbing a hill with Christie-Ann but kept slipping back and getting nowhere. Waking, sweating, uneasy, she thought clearly, guiltily of the time she had defied her mother as a child and been locked out. "When you learn to do as I say, you'll get back in again," her mother had said. Her yells and screams had filled the air in vain. It had become her mother's favourite punishment for a time, till she had learned that day-long, sullen silences had worked almost as well.

She moved now in some agitation and the young sailor said with a grin, "You've been dreaming. Would you like some chocolate?" and she took it and chatted to him in a desultory way till they reached London.

"No, you can't see her. And you should know better than to try."

"I'm not leaving this step till I do." It was Colum's voice and Catherine stepped from the kitchen into the narrow passage, the hands holding the cup and cloth suddenly wringing and trembling and her knees turning to water. Over her mother's head she could just make out Colum's bulk. Dressed in civvies. So after all these weeks in hospital, he must have had his discharge.

She tried to hold her voice steady. "I can't talk to you, Colum."

His face looked pale, unhealthy and the shoulders under the civvie greatcoat appeared thinner, almost skeletal. She could see the anger gather on his features so that her mother, the guardian of the doorway, took an involuntary step backwards. Shambling Boots just happened to be passing the cottage gate at a snail's pace, her face alight with the shining fervour of the gossip on to a good thing. Hastily Lizzie Bathgate opened the door more widely and ordered Colum to come in. He stood at one end of the lobby and Catherine at the other.

"Just let her tell me," he said to Lizzie, "that there's nothing between us any more and I'll go away. But I want to hear it from her."

Catherine advanced up the passageway like someone mesmerized, drawn towards the spot where Colum stood and devouring his face with shocked and tragic eyes.

"Are you all right now?"

"I'm functioning."

"Finished with the Army?"

"Aye. No use to them any more."

"She's wed, as you can see," Lizzie Bathgate intervened. "Happily wed. And the best thing you can do is leave this family alone, and let my lassie better herself."

"Are you happy?" Colum ignored the mother and looked directly at Catherine.

"Does it matter?" she responded. "I *am* married. And that's it. I'm sorry, Colum."

"Can you not leave us alone?" he appealed to Lizzie.

"No, I can't. Say anything you have to say in front of me."

"Just that you should never have done it," he said to Catherine. "You knew— you know—how I feel about you. I thought it was mutual. You can get divorced, you know. I'll wait. He took advantage of you. You were lonely—"

She was weeping now, shaking her head.

"It's over, Colum," she cried. "I wish you nothing but well, but it's over."

"You heard what the lassie said." Standing between them like divine judgement, Lizzie Bathgate folded her arms and addressed herself to her daughter. "Take a hold of yourself," she said savagely. "Do you think you'd ever have made anything of yourself, married to *him*?"

Catherine hunched her shoulders and buried her face in her hands. Colum stood looking at her retreating figure and would have followed her had Lizzie Bathgate not deliberately barred his way. She glared at him like a Gorgon then contemptuously jerked her head towards the door. "There's your way out," she spat. "And don't come back." As Colum hesitated then finally obeyed, he could hear a long, low wailing sob come from Catherine, then the door slammed on his back.

Shambling Boots just "happened" to be passing the gate again as he emerged.

"Keeping better, son?" she enquired. "Just visiting old friends?"

Colum Brodie pushed open the door to the office of the *Courier* and heard the bell give its reassuring old-fashioned tinkle. Splintering rotting floorboards threatened to give way under his tread and the windows had not been cleaned since the last time he was here. There was something intensely reassuring about its determined squalor. He crossed the little vestibule and was into the office, a not over-large room crammed with newspaper files, ledgers, copy, galleys and in the centre of it, at a battered desk, Hallie O'Halloran.

The old man, wizened, bald, like a dusty gnome, peered over steel-rimmed spectacles, grinned, yelped, rose to his feet with hand outstretched.

"You're back!" he greeted. "And not a moment too soon!"

"How're things, Hallie? Doggies and gee-gees been good to you?"

"What do you think?" The old man blinked and wheezed. "Four pages, Colum! That's what they've squeezed us down to. I'm selling. Do you want it? You can have it for a jelly-jar and five clothing coupons. So your war's over, laddie? Aye, well, your troubles are just beginning."

Hallie had always insisted on making the *Courier* tea himself. It was black, thick despite rationing and he'd managed to get condensed milk to sweeten it. Colum sat down and listened to the old man's catalogue of woes. It became clear his head was no longer above water, but what else was new?

It was delicate. Despite his protestations about selling, Hallie was desperately possessive about the *Courier* and dictatorial about how it should be run and had no real intention of handing over to anyone. Colum interjected one or two cautiously innovative ideas about sports coverage and photographs, with Hallie wheezing doubts about the cost.

"There's my gratuity," said Colum at last, "and a bit I've saved. I'll come in with you on a partnership basis, Hallie. You know it makes sense."

The old man gave him a sudden shrewd and calculating look.

"Have they not taken it all off you yet?" he enquired, meaning Colum's parents.

"No. Nor will they, this time." He had the lean and hungry look that Hallie had seen on the faces of young reporters before, but there was a kind of desperation there, that touched an unexpected vein of memory in the old man. He'd come back from the first imbroglio determined to set the heather on fire, open up Dounhead to the fiery strength of his campaigning prose. He remembered what Mabel, his wife, had called it. He was going to be a *magnate*. A magnate! It was a good job she'd kept her sense of humour, poor lass, for they'd struggled instead from hand to mouth and his gambling hadn't improved matters. This young bugger had the same set of silly notions; ignorant as the proverbial pig, green as grass. Hallie

O'Halloran felt a surge of pity for all young men who went away to war and came back determined to make life over into something better. And were pre-destined to fail.

But he liked Colum Brodie. It was difficult to explain—he was just one of those people who were different from everybody else. Nicer, better, kinder. God knows where he got his sensitivity from—not from his graceless family, to be sure. He must be some kind of throw-back, or avatar.

"Would you have a quid on you, Colum? I've got a good 'un for the three-thirty."

In exaggerated martyrdom Colum handed over the money.

"I'll think about the other thing," Hallie promised. "Could you sub up that disgusting report from Councillor Todd, seeing you're here? The eediot canna spell his own name."

"Sure." Colum took off his jacket and sat down as though he'd never been away. O'Halloran looked at him consideringly for a while, then said in a gentle bantering way that precluded any suspicion of nosiness: "So you haven't got yourself married yet?"

"Not yet," said Colum and O'Halloran knew from his tone and expression that he could pry no further.

"Do you know he's got a car now? A navy blue Morris Cowley?"

The two girls had taken the Saturday shopping into a tearoom and Christie-Ann was considering having a cigarette. She had been waiting for this chance to talk to Catherine without their mother hovering in the background, listening. She knew very well what was bothering Catherine. Even since Colum had called at the house to try and see her, she had gone about pale and sometimes red-eyed and looked as though all the energy had been sapped from her. There was no need for Christie-Ann to state who the car-owner was. Colum Brodie had been the unspoken companion in both their thoughts as they queued for sausages and went from one sparsely stocked shop to another in search of goods.

Catherine nodded. "I saw him take his mother out in it."

"You're over him, aren't you?" demanded Christie-Ann desperately. "I mean, you have Edward now and you can't just get unmarried, can you?" To her horror she saw Catherine's eyes brim up with tears.

"Oh, I'm over him," said Catherine vehemently. "And I have Edward, don't I?" She managed a strained little smile. "Don't get me wrong. I like Edward. He's been good to me. I see everything Mother said to me is true: I can have a good and settled life. But the truth is . . ."

"Yes, what is the truth?" demanded Christie-Ann in a horror-stricken voice, as though she denied it before it was spoken.

"The truth is I want Colum. I've always wanted him and things like having money and being comfortable don't seem to matter a damn if I can't have him."

"What is it," demanded Christie-Ann, in a hypnotized voice, "that makes him so special?"

"I don't know, Kissie." The childhood endearment slipped out unconsciously. "He just seems to me to be different from everybody else. To have a special quality of loving-kindness that doesn't judge people. A way of looking at things that isn't critical. He could have gone away from here, but he won't cut himself off from his family, whatever people say about them—"

"He's got a touch of the poet." Christie-Ann nodded vehemently. "I know what you mean. I feel it too."

"In the beginning, I mean when we first —I never felt cold, Kissie. I felt like 1 was a plant put out in the sun, ready to open and bloom. It's so hard to explain. It was like being on a different plane and there were all sorts of possibilities to life, when I was with him."

"But not when you are with Edward?"

Catherine shook her head. "I waited for it. There was a little spurt at the beginning, of hope, I mean. But after that it was as though I wanted to pull back all the time. I made a foolish miscalculation and now I think I must undo it, Kissie. I have to undo it or I think I shall go mad."

The look of open horror did not leave Christie-Ann's expression as the two girls paid for their tea and set off for home. She saw that Catherine got up as though she were a sleep-walker and that she walked into the table edge without feeling it. When she spoke to Catherine in the bus, her sister did not answer, but turned towards her a face full of such desperation that Christie-Ann could find no words to counteract it.

Lizzie Bathgate had been resting in front of the fire but sensed something was amiss as the girls came in without any form of greeting.

"What's up?"

"Ask Catherine," said Christie-Ann. "You were the one who wanted her to marry Edward Elkins. See for yourself what you've done."

Catherine sat down on the hard chair by the door. "I want to leave him," she said.

"Has she met that other one?" demanded Lizzie of Christie-Ann.

"I presume you mean Colum? No, she hasn't been meeting him. She doesn't need to. She knows she still loves him."

"Is this true?"

"It is."

"You don't need to ask!" Christie-Ann broke in bitterly. "You know well enough how she's always felt about him—"

"Then why did you bring Edward

Elkins home here?" Lizzie demanded of her elder daughter.

"Out of—out of nothing more than a wish to be friends. With someone billeted in a strange place."

"You tell me you don't want to get on? You didn't fancy the idea of a man with a degree and a cultivated mind? You hung on his every word for a while. 'Edward says this. Edward says that'."

"That's all it was—intellectual curiosity. How many are there the likes of Edward in Dounhead?"

"But she doesn't love him," said Christie-Ann.

"You have taken your vows in the church," said Lizzie. "What are folk going to say if you run out on your man now? Him a soldier away in the army?" Her mouth hardened. "You are learning something we all have to come to terms with, my lassie. You have made your bed so you'll lie on it."

"Reverend, can I ask you something?"

The Reverend Thomas Macwhirter looked uncertainly at the trim, neat figure on his doorstep. A faint blur of pink hat and veiling rose up in his memory. This visitor's wedding, a year ago.

"Come in, Catherine. It's remaining cold, isn't it?" He blew on his bloodless fingers and led the way into a chilly study. "About the sale of work, is it? We're always greatly indebted to your mother's skill with the needle."

"No." She sat down on the visitor's chair, gazing at him across the cluttered desk. "It's about my marriage."

"Yes?" His attention sharpened.

"It should never have taken place." She took a handkerchief from her coat pocket and dabbed her eyes, fighting for composure.

The Reverend looked at the ceiling. Needed whitening. A wife who blew hot and cold about conjugal rights and this tidy, usually dependable person opposite looking to him for advice. He reminded himself it was part of his ministry.

"Har. You've been married how long?"

"A little over a year."

"You have met someone else?"

"No." The voice trembled.

"But you have seen little of your husband in that time."

"Only on leave. It's been often enough. I should never have married him. I don't love him."

"You have been having difficulties, I presume, on the physical side?"

She looked at him with the first glimmering of hope, but embarrassed beyond bearing. "Yes. I've got so I don't want him to touch me."

"That must distress him very much."

"Yes." A pause.

"It isn't fair to him. He's a good man. He actually loves me. But I want to be free. I'd rather be divorced than living some kind of a lie. How do I get a divorce, Reverend?"

He gave a grim smile.

"Steady on. I need hardly remind you, Catherine, you took your vows before God. You have no grounds for divorce. You have not given this marriage of yours a chance."

"Do you think not, Reverend?" she asked pitiably.

"Of course not. Wartime marriages start off under a terrible strain. Nothing is normal. You see your partner for a couple of days, then it's letters only—and often

49

not very many of them—for months on end."

"But about love, Reverend."

"Catherine, I have to remind you about what our Lord said about love. It is long-suffering and kind."

"You can't advise me about divorce, then?"

"I could not possibly. In all conscience. When children come, a marriage settles down—"

"I don't want children." Her voice rose.

He looked at her exasperatedly. He did have a sermon to finish and it had been going reasonably well, before she arrived.

"Have you talked about this with your mother?"

There was a long silence, while she sat with her head to one side. "Catherine? Have you?"

"She thinks I'm wicked."

"Try again. She can give you some comfort."

"No. It's impossible."

"Then I think you know what course you must take. But pray, Catherine. More things are wrought by prayer than you think."

"I am past praying."

"Then I cannot help you."

She rose, dry-eyed once again. Macwhirter thought what a very tidy girl she was. Modest, well-dressed. Neat but not gaudy, as Wesley had put it. Excellent wife material, on the face of it.

"What is the matter with you, Miss Bathgate?" The foreman who had known the family for years still called her respectfully by her maiden name. "You've passed inferior work again. God, it can mean life or death to some poor sap in an airyplane."

"I'm sorry." He seemed to waver up and down before her eyes and she put a hand to steady herself on her workbench. The man said concernedly. "Are you all right, lass?"

"A bit faint."

He summoned over one of the turbanned girls who were watching. "Take Miss Bathgate here up to the nurse. Get her a cup of tea or something."

"Is it the curse?" Jean Buchanan steered Catherine away from the factory floor towards the quiet of the offices. "Or maybe the want of it, Catherine? Maybe you're in the family way."

Catherine shook her head fiercely. "No. It's not that. I'm just tired."

The nurse sent her home with instructions to see her doctor. He diagnosed anaemia, pleurisy triggered off by a recent cold and prescribed rest and treatment. At the end of three weeks, he suggested munitions work was too strenuous for her and she should have a period of rest.

"Nothing much wrong with you that seeing your man again wouldn't cure, am I right?" he joked then. Her mother said they would miss the money.

It wasn't her husband she was thinking of most of the time. It was how it had been for Colum and herself when the magic had worked.

"What did you say to your mother?" he had asked.

"I told her I was going to watch the former pupils' hockey match. What did you say to yours?"

"I didn't need to say anything. They don't bother. They'll say when I get in tonight. 'Where have you been?' and I'll say 'Around and about' and they'll leave it at that."

"It isn't like that in our house."

He took her hand. Together they stared through the frost-rimed windows of the little country bus. Away on either side stretched fields and furrows hardened with frost and delicately dusted with snow. They looked at each other with pleasure. "Isn't it lovely?" she said, shivering. "You'd think it was enamelled."

When they got off the bus several miles on she stared around at a Lanarkshire that was not familiar. Little towns and hamlets had gradually thinned and this was country, good and proper. You had to search the landscape for habitation and that was no more than the occasional farm or ploughman's cottage tucked into a fold in the land or a sheltering arbour of trees.

"Was there a pit here once?" she demanded, unbelievingly. He turned her round and pointed out the undulating hump of a bing. A broken stump of winding machinery confirmed his claim.

He walked her along the road towards the bing and as they turned a corner there were suddenly about a dozen broken-down cottages, a pit row, set back only yards from the roadside. Empty. Breaking up. The roofs caving in, windows broken, joinery split by frost, rain and possibly tramps. Except for the last one, which still appeared to be reasonably intact, with curtains at the window and paint applied within the past year or two on the door and windows.

He took a key from his pocket and admitted them. "I used to come every Saturday," he said, "and run my grannie's messages."

"She lived here all alone?"

"She was used to the country."

"When did she die?"

"Last year. In the county hospital. My folks could use the furniture—" he gestured round the room they had entered immediately from the doorway—"but it's getting the transport for it. Good job it's here though, isn't it? For us. Sit down there and I'll light a fire."

She thought in the years afterwards that no-one had the capacity to release simple happiness in her like Colum. Why was that? When he looked at her something kindled in his eyes and lit candles in her.

He was as she thought human beings should be in their perfect state—totally receptive, totally non-judgemental, totally forgiving. When she was with him she was Catherine in a way she was not elsewhere. Her laughter, her voice, had a different ring. She was without self-consciousness, or rigidity, graceful and free.

Had it something to do with the way he looked? Or the way he felt about her? As to the first, he was rangy and loose-limbed, giving the impression of a full physical awareness of what was going on, a readiness to join in, participate and above all celebrate the quirks and surprises of daily living. His dark hair, she always thought, really did tumble. It was a tangle. It shaped his head in strangely classical and poetic fashion, so that he didn't look like any other man in Dounhead and his straight nose compounded this enigmatic, ready-made dignity that could never be taken away from him, that made people ready to listen to him and pay attention.

And as to how he felt about her . . . She did for him what he did for her, aroused a total and joyous response, a conviction that she would understand everything about him, so he could tell her everything, good as well as the bad. How he felt about his father, the sometimes murderous anger because he drank and beat his mother, alongside the familial loyalty that found excuses for him, that knew how long ambition had broken him, how vanishing dreams had twisted him. To Catherine he could admit the shame he and his brothers and sisters felt when the parental rows got out of hand and became recklessly public, when debts could not be paid and food could not be bought. And the amazing thing was she had found exactly the right note to strike, had been able to accept everything he told her without shock or repugnance because he might have to live among the destruction but he was no part of it. He was going to rise above it, a phoenix from the ashes, free others as he would free himself, just as she was going to break away from her own harsher colder poverty and find warmth and love and security.

That was how it had been, that magical afternoon when they had travelled to his grandmother's derelict pit row cottage, knowing they were going somewhere from which there would be no return. Both a little afraid, both unaccustomed to lying about their movements, but knowing there was a country that had to be explored, a consummation that had to have its time.

"Is this all there is?" she asked, looking round the pit cottage. He nodded. "It's a single-end. One small room. She brought up six children here. The WC is out the back."

Two beds set into the wall. By the front window, a big double sink. In the wall opposite the beds, a steel range that had once blazed with free coal, sparking and raging now with the logs and coal lumps Colum had found in a bunker outside. The mantelpiece bore two wally dugs and a tea caddy with the name Lipton, with behind it a dusty wooden crucifix because Colum's grandmother had been Catholic though married to a Protestant.

He pushed the kettle down on the flames while she laid out the thick crockery that indicated this had been a family of big hungry sons with a mother who had given up all pretensions of gentility. Had she hoped for something finer, with roses on it, the grandmother?

Catherine felt a tender affection for the unknown old woman, because she had stroked Colum's tangled hair, sent him to the Co-op with tokens instead of money to buy a quarter of boiled ham and two ounces of strippit balls, put iodine on his scabby knees. Here he'd got the affection so seldom on hand at home.

They were very formal, sitting on either side of the table with its brown chenille cover, eating the teabread they'd brought with them, drinking the milkless tea.

"Will there be a war?"

"Sure to be. How else do they get rid of the surplus men, the unemployed?"

"Will you go?"

"I'll have to."

Two spectres, then, there had been in the single-end that day. The grandmother and her loving-kindness, now in the past; the war, whose impending shadow grew with the days. And then the snow had come to enchant the present, turning the room into a cosy cavern, magical as Aladdin's cave, where their looks were the jewels, their breath the velvet that lined the walls.

Happiness. Not asked for. Sprung on them like a tender trap.

"Let me do it, Catherine. Say you will."

Beyond all reason. "Yes, oh yes. Oh yes, yes, yes."

It was rain, with sleet beginning to mix in. Dounhead was merging with the mist and the rain, draining into the landscape except for the main street where a few determined souls hurried to the picture house to see the latest Joan Crawford.

"You're not going out on such a night," her mother said. "After having the pleurisy."

"I feel like a walk," Catherine said.

"Hell mend you if you get sick again." It was her way, Catherine thought, of being caring.

She put the scarf round her head and pulled the hood of her raincoat up over that. She didn't even take an umbrella, it was too much of a struggle to keep it up against the wind that always scourged the streets, none of its vigour lost on its journey across the Ayrshire and Lanarkshire moors from the Atlantic. In a little she began to feel her weakness, but she kept on. She walked round the crescent in the slum clearance where the Brodies lived twice until, with the blackout dark fast approaching, she unsnecked the gate and walked up the garden path to the battered front door.

It was his mother who answered. "Yes?"

"Can I speak to Colum?"

"What would you be wanting to see him about?"

"A private matter, Mrs. Brodie." Her chest ached with unshed tears.

He came through from the kitchen then, his face unbelieving, still eating his tea.

"Catherine? What can I do for you?"

"Can I speak to you?"

"There's the front room," conceded Bridget Brodie unwillingly.

"Go in there if you like. The blackout'll be on us in a minute."

The room was barely furnished, with cheap Utility armchairs and a battered piano but a few daffodils graced a cheap glass vase. He closed the door carefully behind them and motioned her to sit down. She was glad to. She sat on the edge of one of the rexine chairs, pulling her skirt nervously over her knees. He waited.

"Colum," she began, "I came to try and explain."

The door opened a fraction and the face of the youngest Brodie, Kathleen, appeared round it. It was grubby, streaked with tears and she had lost the ribbon out of her hair.

"What's she doin' here?" she demanded.

"Shut the door, Kathleen," said Colum. The child came in instead of going out. "You're a bad disobedient girl," said her brother angrily.

"Come here, Kathleen," said Catherine. "Listen, if I give you a toffee—" she felt in her raincoat pocket and produced it— "will you go out and leave us in peace?"

The child smirked at her shyly, but nodded. "Away you go then," Catherine urged. "I just want to talk to Colum a minute."

"Speak then," he said. "You've got your chance."

"I married Edward because I liked him. I wanted to turn away from all the damage that you and me going together caused our families. Let's face it, Colum, your mother doesn't like me and mine doesn't like you."

The door opened and a disreputable urchin with oversized short trousers and gappy socks falling over dirty sandshoes came in and stood grinning at them. "Go away, Liam," said Colum.

"I want a toffee."

Catherine produced one and the door closed again.

"I'm getting my own place," said Colum. "A flat. Away from here. Got to get peace to write."

"You still romanticizing over being a writer?"

"Sure." He smiled at her at last. "Don't tell anybody. They'll think I'm a loonie."

"No," she said. "No. You're not. You go ahead and write."

He fell silent again, then volunteered into the embarrassed vacuum, "It's hard to know what to say, you a married woman and all."

"It didn't stop you coming to try and see me."

"No."

"And when we met in the station . . . I

couldn't get over how glad I was to see you."

"It doesn't explain how you came to marry him."

"I quite liked him. I didn't know how to handle it. Colum—" she sought desperately for the right words—"I wanted to get away from feeling sad, from feeling nothing was ever going to work out. I thought your family would cling on to you forever—they need you to sort things out, to steady them. They can't spare you."

"You can't pretend your mother didn't have a hand in it."

"No, I can't pretend. She and Edward worked on me together. She kept saying her mind would be at rest, knowing I had a man who would always look after me right. She never had that, you know, Colum. My father was next door to a wastrel."

"She was trying to get something for you that was really for herself."

"Ah, well, don't criticize her. She's known the day she had no bread to put in our mouths. It came down to poverty, Colum. Poverty was what I was frightened of getting into with you, just when it looked as though I might be able to climb out of it myself."

"You think things like houses matter, then? Houses and things to put in them? Fancy clothes?"

"I do. I think dignity matters and you don't have that if you're forever scraping round for a copper to buy bread."

"A sell-out, was it, then?" he demanded, with a hardening face. "You're telling me I'm not good enough for you."

"You know it's not that. But I do want security. I want my self-respect."

"Why are you here then, Catherine?"

She looked away from him. Tears began to course down her face and she did nothing to stem them. "I don't know why."

"It solves nothing." There was a note of rage and desperation in his voice that turned her face once again towards him. They looked at each other with a desolate resignation. "I can't say to you, write to the poor bugger and tell him it's finished. I've seen Dear Johns destroy a man."

"Then why did you come to our house? Tell me I could get a divorce? I couldn't, you know. I've no grounds."

"I came because I felt then how you feel now. But better counsel has to prevail. We've got to behave like decent human beings, not savages, all instinct and nothing else."

She rose then, drying her eyes. She went over to him and touched his cheek. "Yes," she said. "Shall we let the past go?"

"I've no doubt," he responded, "you'll become a rich lady, Catherine. With all the dignity and respect you want."

3

"**Y**OU'RE not going out tonight."
Lizzie Bathgate turned the back door key in the lock and then extracted it. "It's no use looking. I've got the front door key as well."

"You can't do this to me." Christie-Ann faced her mother furiously.

She had just come downstairs wearing a pretty blue and white voile dress, blue suède courts and her hair tied up in a blue ribbon with a chenille snood. She carried a jacket of grey fake fur over one arm.

"Where was it you were going?"

"I've told you. An office party, for a young fellow that's been called up."

"What's his name?"

"Tom. Tom Harrison."

"I've never heard tell of him."

"I don't know him very well. It doesn't matter. The whole office is going."

"Well, you're no'."

The girl sat down at the kitchen table, her face crumpling.

"When you told me you were going to Hawktoun last week, you were in Glasgow with Sarah Rankin."

"Who told you that?" Christie-Ann's rosy face jerked up.

"Her own mother. Sarah got off wi' some Yank. Glasgow's hoaching with them."

"We just went to the pictures. We met Rose Paterson and she said there were queues for the 'Mark of Zorro' in Hawktoun, so we went to see Anna Neagle in Glasgow."

"You never saw fit to tell your own mother."

"Do I have to tell you everything?"

"No. And I don't have to let you go out and make a fool of yourself with some Yank."

"I never went with a Yank."

"Nor will you."

"Mother—I have to go. Sarah will be waiting for me."

"She can wait."

Deliberately, Lizzie put the door key in her battered black leather handbag, poked the fire and sat down with some sewing and a bag of peppermints.

67

Christie-Ann looked at her hopelessly. After some minutes, the picture of dejection, she climbed the stairs to her own room.

Once there, she began to fiddle with the catch of the sash window. Carefully, without a sound, she lifted the window and looked out, a plan formulating in her mind. If she could get a foothold in the lilac tree, it was no distance to the ground. She put her fur jacket on, tied a headscarf round her hair—and climbed out.

"Christie-Ann? What are you doing out at this time of night?"

"As you can see. Walking home."

Colum Brodie had been to a council meeting that had run late and there had been few people about as he drove home. A light evening mist had descended but the trudging figure of Christie-Ann had not been all that difficult to identify in front of his dimmed headlights. He opened the car door now and said, "Get in. I'll drive you to the corner of your street."

"It was foggy, coming from Glasgow," she volunteered. "It took forever, what with the blackout and all."

"Won't they be worried at home?"

"They don't know I'm out."

He looked more closely at her and saw her face looked strained and anxious. He let the car slow down and then stop in an inlet of road.

"Christie-Ann?" he said questioningly.

The girl burst out like a pent-up dam. "She won't do to me what she did to Catherine, Colum. My mother, I mean, I won't let her ruin my life! I'll run away. I hate her!"

"No, you don't hate her," he said quietly. "I might. But don't you hate. You're too young for hate."

"I'm too young for everything," she said sulkily.

"Come on," he abjured. "What's the use of feeling sorry for yourself?"

"It's been nothing but Catherine in our house, you know. For ages. Catherine's not well. Catherine's in a mood. What about Christie-Ann? Do I not have an identity, too? Don't I matter?"

"How is she?" he asked bleakly. "The famous Catherine. The former Miss Bathgate?"

"Edward's coming home on leave. She's

hoping he'll agree and let her start the commercial college she's always talking about. She's got a friend, Mary Mackinnon, that lost her husband in the Air Force, coming in with her. They're out most days trying to scrounge second-hand typewriters wherever they can. You can't get them for love nor money."

"So she means to make a go of it?"

"She will. That's something you have to recognize about our Catherine. She has a dead practical streak."

"And do you think she'll make a go of it with him?"

"With Edward? I don't know. She's got to, hasn't she?" She gazed at him a little timidly. "I think she should have waited till you got back, Colum." She held his gaze. "I would have done."

He shifted in his seat, pulling his tweed coat about him. "Come on, my girl, we'd better get you home. How will you get in without being heard?"

"The way I got out. By the rone-pipe and the lilac tree. I left a bolster in my bed in case anyone peeked in."

His mouth tweaked at the corners in spite of himself. "What a way to go on! It must have been all those *Girl's Crystals* you've been reading!"

"Not a word," she pleaded. "And let me off before the corner of the street. What they don't see round here isn't worth seeing."

"O.K. Glad to have been of service."

She got out but came back and stuck her head through the car window. "Colum," she said huskily, "what you have to remember about our Catherine is that she felt it worst of all when we had to go on the parish. When my mother had to queue with derelicts for clothes and shoes. Neither my mother nor Catherine ever got over it. I was too young. Not that I would have cared. My father gave his health in the last war for his King and Country and what did they ever do for him? I'm harder mettle. But they have this —this pride. Do you see?"

"Go home, girl, or you'll be for it."

She went. He peered into the misty dark till her jaunty, straight-backed figure disappeared then let in the gears and drove thoughtfully on.

He had never paid all that much attention to Catherine's younger sister till now, but he had to acknowledge she was growing into a really attractive young woman. Her face was very like her sister's, yet it had the stamp of a totally different, more buoyant personality. There was a lot of gaiety and defiance in her, where Catherine was pressed in, reserved, with something of a core of iron in her when it came to making her mark.

Her sympathy for him had touched him. It warmed him now and he let it settle in his veins because just recently everything seemed to have been touched by tension and uncertainty. His coming home had unsettled his father, who had been belligerent about his demob cash and had wanted it doled out to him so that he could spend it in the pub. He had been cold and determined about it: the old man wasn't going to touch a penny of it. He helped his mother where he could, but even she spent money foolishly, as though she'd never seen it before and didn't know its value, which was half-true. He and Lucille had decided they would pay the rent between them, see the young children were shod, but their parents regarded their terms as Draconian and waged perpetual nagging war for hand-outs.

He could have left Dounhead for good, gone south in search of better opportunities; even, because so many journalists were called up, found something lowly in Fleet Street. Hallie O'Halloran had taught him the rudiments of subbing, had taught him to look at what he wrote with a spare and judgemental eye. "Throw out your darlings," he would say, meaning dispense with the flowery turns of phrase, the fancy perorations, for which in any case there was no room in truncated wartime pages. But when Colum turned in a well-written piece for the back page, an essay on country matters, say, or a humorous piece about the rigours of rationing, or a dialogue that captured the hidden nuances of Lowland speech, the old man's face would glow with pleasure. He wouldn't say anything, but his hand would land on Colum's shoulder, he would test him out on some new and difficult assignment, he would chortle with unrestrained professional pleasure.

Why *did* he stay? He had given the matter a lot of thought but he hadn't arrived at an answer. Because *she* was there, in Dounhead, her bright head sometimes in his vision as it was often in his mind? Because something wanted him to make a stand as his father's son, to retrieve the name of Brodie? When he went into the *Courier* office he felt at home, half of the little empire was his. And when he wanted to talk about books and writers, Hallie was there to listen and encourage. He hadn't cared much for England, he felt his bones and marrow belonged in the dour Lowland enclave that was Dounhead, that his roots went down into the dark of its coalmines and political dissent, yes, even into its poverty and indistinguished but also unrelinquished struggle.

When Catherine had wanted to tease him, when they had laid bare what they were about in their innermost souls, she had said he had a touch of the poet. If that was so, it was Dounhead, dirty urchins, street corner boys, old women in shawls, targes in flowered overalls, scabby picture houses, religious bigots, hardened attitudes that had given it to him. His metaphor for this was a grubby bent daffodil pushing its way up in a slum clearance garden, while heedless children kicked footballs over it, muddied it, smeared its clear yellow but could not quite obliterate it. Dounhead's image could not rise to anything more than this, but it was something, it persisted. He half-smiled at himself in the dark of the car, amused at his own deliberations.

His pleasure in seeing Christie-Ann lingered a little longer, but was gradually superseded by the memory of Catherine's sadness when he had last seen her. Her need to be loved had been there as blatantly as her suppression of it. A faint perfume lingered in the car—what was it? Wallflower, perhaps. He realized Christie-Ann must have worn it but so had Catherine, on high days and holidays. Never too much, for it was not in her to be indiscreet. As the thought of her entered his body like a familiar ache he put it away from him forcibly. He had let her down by being what he was, from a poor and looked-down-on family. Ah no, ah no, no more of that. He concentrated on the Council report he had to summarize before bed.

Edward Elkins, home on embarkation leave, looked away from Catherine in rueful resignation.

"It would soon go out of fashion, if it was like that every time."

"I'm sorry."

"Is there somebody else?"

"What do you take me for?"

He got up and dressed. She pulled the blankets up to her chin and watched him.

"I've—I've been ill," she said. "You've got to make allowances. And there's been all this work at the college."

"Are you sure you want to do it?"

"I don't want to be a stay-at-home cabbage."

"Most women would be happy enough to be simple housewives, but if you want to work, I won't prevent it."

"We're calling it Miss Bathgate's Commercial College. Mary thinks that sounds best."

"Why not Mrs. Elkins' College?"

"Hasn't the same ring."

He came and sat on the bed, taking her

right hand and bending back the fingers like a sadistic boy, till she gave a little cry of pain.

"Don't, Edward!"

"It's been college, college, college, Mary, Mary, Mary the whole leave."

"I didn't know you were coming. We've got to be ready for the opening."

"You don't really care for me, do you? Not the way I love you."

"You overwhelm me."

He allowed himself to sag against her, his head into her shoulder and presently she was aware that he might have been crying.

"Edward!"

"We might never have time."

She said softly, "Then that's the war's doing, none of mine." But her hands were gentle as they brushed his hair away from his face. "We have a lot of talking and understanding to do, Edward, but it'll have to wait. At least when you're away you can think: she's too busy working to get up to mischief." She raised one eyebrow not uncomically and he grinned at last and held her to him.

"I love you so much. I don't know what

would happen to me if you found somebody else."

He waited for her denial or for a tight-
ening of her arms around him. Neither
happened. She seemed to have gone off in
a kind of trance-like state of absorption.

"You'll write regularly? Don't worry if
you don't hear from me straight away.
You'll get the letters eventually."

"Of course I'll write."

"And don't get ill again. Take care of
yourself."

He waited, then mimicked her voice:
"*And you take care of yourself, Edward.
Don't go stopping any nasty German
bullets.*"

"It goes without saying."

"Kiss me."

She did. But after a few moments he let
his arms fall by his sides and got up and
continued with his packing.

"Hallie! Did you hear the news on the
wireless? We've done it at last. The troops
are on their way into France. The Second
Front at last!"

Colum Brodie crashed into the *Courier*
office with the face of an excited

schoolboy. Everybody had known it would happen sooner or later but it had been a year of hope deferred, of sickening hearts, of the bombing intensified in the South.

Hallie was sitting behind his desk as usual. As usual it resembled a bomb site; galleys, copy, broken pencils, pipes, ashtrays. But there was something different. The old man's face was grey. His movements as he lit his pipe were puppet-like, drawn by strings.

"Something up?" He toned down his exuberance, thinking Hallie would say a folding machine broken down, a story missed. Instead the old editor said, "I've got to get back to the wife. We heard this morning—"

"What, for God's sake, Hallie?"

"Oor Helen and her weans. Doon in London. One of thae flying bombs."

"Ah no." He could feel the waves of sickness hit him, the denial break his composure, the rage mount up in his chest. Helen had been a gentle, ugly, happy girl.

"Oh, but aye," said Hallie, brokenly. "My lass and her bairns. A' three o' them." He rose automatically. "You'll take over, Colum. I have to get back to the wife, you understand."

"I'll run you back. I'll do everything that needs doing, Hallie. You don't need to worry about a thing."

"You're a good lad, Colum."

"I thought they lived outside London."

"No' far enough outside, it seems."

"The bastards. Thank Christ we're on their tail at last."

Usually his father slept in till midday, got up, drank what tea was left in the teapot, no matter what state or temperature then joined his cronies at the Miners' Welfare, street corner or the public-house. Colum had not spoken to him for weeks, not because he didn't want to but because his father made himself inaccessible. The last conversation had admittedly been a heated one and had involved Colum in warning his father against raising his hand to his mother.

Now the young man diffidently pushed open the door of Tolley's pub and approached his father, a solitary figure standing with one foot on the brass rail. Donald Brodie wore a thread-bare navy suit, a tweed cap at a jaunty angle and the grubby white silk-type scarf which for some reason all young miners had once adopted as off-duty wear, maybe in contrast to the coal-stiffened rags in which they passed their working lives.

He gave a start when he saw Colum.

"Aye, there," he offered cautiously.

"What you having, Father?"

"Hauf and hauf," said the older man, immediately, meaning a small whisky and a beer chaser. "Since you're asking."

Colum ordered the same for himself. There was something different about him, his father judged. A cockiness. He waited.

"They've asked me to take over the *Courier*."

"Who have?"

"The O'Hallorans. I'm putting my gratuity into it and buying over the machinery by degrees. I thought it might amuse you, to know your son was on his way to being a filthy capitalist."

Brodie spat into the sawdust at his feet. It was so long since he had communicated with his family except by drunken bawling that he was plainly discomfited and lost for words. "Aye, you'll be a' right," he said eventually. He drank down his beer and appeared to feel the better for it.

"You'll no' want to know your old man now," he challenged. "I had a dream once, you know. It was to run pits that didn't take the stuffing out a man. See where it got me. A near-broken back and empty pockets." He turned one of his trouser pockets inside out to illustrate the case.

"If you kept off the hard stuff," suggested Colum mildly, knowing better than to go further.

Donald Brodie called over the barman, a small, neat Irishman with black eyes set closely together, and said, "Pat here is my pal. Aren't you, pal? He knows. You know, don't you, Pat?"

Not quite certain what knowledge he was supposed to possess, the barman nonetheless nodded affably. "Aye, that'll be right, Donald. Right enough."

"Same again, Pat," said Brodie. "My son here is paying."

"You should try," Colum essayed again, as they supped the second whisky, "to keep out of pubs for my mother's sake. When I'm in funds, Da, I'll get a specialist to look at your back."

"I took them on," said Donald Brodie, his mind running along some obscure need to *show*—show what? He had lost sight of whatever it was as soon as grasped but he held Colum's arm the better to demonstrate *something*. "I took the pit bosses on in my day. In *my* day. I'm no' finished yet, son. You'll see." He moved slightly to one side and staggered just a little. "Pat, set them up again."

Colum stood his ground. He had been so overwhelmed by the sense of destiny when he'd worked out the *Courier* deal—Hallie was retiring from the scene completely following a slight stroke caused by his daughter's death—that he'd felt able to take on anything. Even momentarily the reform and rejuvenation of his father. But the drab pub, the slow working of his father's mind, his pale, debauched face brought him up short.

He had to make the paper work, but now all his shortcomings as regards experience were catching up with him in his mind. He should have got out of this place and started somewhere fresh. His father looked at him with rheumy, pleading eyes.

Whatever Donald wanted, he couldn't supply it. It was too late.

"Do you fancy a night at the dogs?" Maybe all he could offer was affection, a night of diversion. Maybe if he and his father had one last drink together, he would get over this awful hollowness in his bowels. How did anyone ever know they could make it?

"So is it true what I heard? That you're running the *Courier* on your own now?"

Christie-Ann had met Colum on her way home from work. She was at the munitions factory now, having been called up soon after her birthday. It had been a hot day, the turbans the girls wound round their hair for safety, hot and constricting and the "Music while you Work" for once unwelcome in the clattering heat. Her face was streaked with grime and she held her blackened hands self-consciously behind her back.

"You know what happened to old man O'Halloran? Bit of a stroke after his daughter was killed. I'm buying him out." He could not hide the expression of mild pride.

"Oh, quite the tycoon." She teased.

"Do you like the munitions? Look at the sight of you!"

She blushed underneath the grime. "I like the money."

"Been climbing out any more windows these nights?"

She shook her head. "I wouldn't dare."

"Not a natural rebel then, are you?"

She shook her head again, but then laughed a little wryly and said, "I wouldn't say that. But what's the use?"

"Every use," he said, upbraidingly, maintaining her embarrassed gaze with his own steady one. "Everyone has a right to their own life and don't you forget it, Christie-Ann."

"Is it a sermon you're giving me?"

"No, just a timely reminder of the nature of the Scottish mother." He began to walk off, then came back impulsively and handed her a ticket from his jacket pocket.

"What is it?" she demanded, taking it.

"Just a seat at the Roxy pictures. They come in for free to the office. It's Veronica Lake this week. You might enjoy it."

"Just the one ticket?"

"I might use the other."

"Why give it to me? Lucille might like it."

"Because I like you."

"Do you?"

"I do. Especially with oil on your nose."

"I know." She took the light-hearted teasing in the spirit it was given. "There's nothing like a hot session with an oily spanner for making you irresistible."

She wondered if he would turn up the same night when she went to the pictures. In the event he did, but it was half way through the main feature and he did no more than give her a friendly nod. Before the second feature came on, there was a Pathé newsreel, mainly about the war in Europe.

She said, "You know Catherine's husband's gone? To the Second Front?"

"It'll all be over now," he said, with heavy irony. "I wonder if Hitler knows."

"Don't be like that," she abjured him.

"I saw her the other day," he said, as though he didn't want to talk about it but could not help himself. She watched his eyes in the dark, close to her own face and saw them dilate with a kind of painful pressure. "She doesn't change much. Still goes about with that frail imperiousness of hers that never fails to get me, right in the solar plexus."

"Does it hurt?"

"Naw-aw." He denied it.

"Don't let it." She patted his arm as it lay on the moquette fauteille and then let her hand lie there. He brought his other hand over and grasped it. The hands moved and writhed in each other for long seconds, then fell apart. She could hear his breathing. It was almost stertorous, and she dreaded that he might weep.

"It's all right," she whispered, her own breath hurting in her chest. His head came over and buried itself for a moment in her hair.

"When do you think it changed?" demanded Christie-Ann. "The way you felt about me?"

They were sitting in the back of the Morris Cowley, near the banks of the river on the stretch between Hawktoun and Dounhead, a spot much frequented by lovers. It was dark and a pale moon filtered through the nearby trees.

Colum moved uneasily. He had to be nudged towards analysis, declaration, all the time. He lifted a strand of her soft hair and said "I suppose that night going home from the pictures."

"Yes." She leant against his shoulder, sighed and smiled. "Our first kiss."

"I'm not sure I meant it to happen," he admitted, but kissing her brow for re-assurance.

"But you couldn't stop it." She wriggled against him. "Any more than we can stop it now."

She put up her hands and drew his face down to hers. "Oh, Col, I do love you the most anyone ever loved any-body." He responded, half-laughing, half-embarrassed by her vehemence.

"But it's probably ill-advised." He pushed her gently away from him. The eyes that were so like Catherine's gazed back at him. From the face that was so like Catherine's.

"How can it be? When it feels so right?"

"You know. As well as I do."

Her lower lip came out and angry tears sprang up in her eyes. But she said it in a calm enough voice. "Am I to be haunted by her? By my own sister? She's married now. She's made it clear how she feels. Col, we can start afresh and make our own life. I don't care what my mother says. I am *me*. Not Catherine. I can stand up for my rights."

"Maybe the best thing would have been for me to go away from here."

"But why? Your livelihood is here. Going away doesn't change anything."

"By God, if we come out in the open, it'll give the gossips a field day. Not to mention your mother."

"But we decided we weren't going to be like that. Pay attention to the whisperers and street-corner hags. What do they matter?"

"In a place like Dounhead, they do."

"Not really." But she sounded deflated. After a pause, she said, as if trying him out, "Maybe it's me who should go away. I dare say you'd like that."

"Maybe you should."

The angry silence lay between them. After a time, she opened the door of the car and got out. Walking down to the river's edge, she looked around for something to throw in the water. Little flat stones came to hand. She skimmed them expertly. Presently, he came and joined her. Looking for stones. Skimming them, too, though not any more expertly.

At last he took her arm and pulled her towards him, gazing down in the moon's shallow glimmer at her tight, angry face.

"I think we *should* stop seeing each other."

"Very well."

"Get in the car, I'll see you home."

"I'll walk, thank you."

"It's too far."

Over the stones, up the grass, into the car. Christie-Ann weeping quietly, Colum with a hang-dog face. And then in the car, the dark reconciliation when something was unleashed that neither of them could put a name to, but that was yearning, a hurting, a need to overcome. Something that would not be resolved, that kept them out later, arguing, making-up. And so it was each time they met.

"To be able to buy your own house outright," said Lizzie Bathgate, "is something any young married woman would give her right arm for."

"Well, I gave five hundred pounds," said Catherine. "Do you like it?"

Lizzie walked from the empty lounge back into the green and yellow kitchen. "It'll do," she said, with satisfaction. "Once we've done it up. John Armour the auctioneer says prices will rise again once the war is over. You've got a bargain."

They looked through the curtainless windows at the rain-sodden back garden. It was long, neat and with a garden shed at the foot and it also encompassed the house, which was detached, greystone, formal. The wide paths were laid with white chips. Not at all the sort of house you'd expect a young woman to choose, Christie-Ann was thinking privately. When she left home she wanted a modern flat, done up in beige and cream and with no fussy pictures on the walls. Still, Catherine was looking a bit happier now the decision had been made. She might be lonely here, till Edward came home, but at least she would be her own woman, away from their mother's jurisdiction. Christie-Ann heaved a sigh of mournful envy.

"What's up with you?" Lizzie demanded sharply.

"Nothing. I was just wondering, Catherine? Will you go for Utility furniture or second-hand?"

"Good second-hand," said Lizzie Bathgate promptly, not noticing that Christie-Ann's question had not been addressed to her. She was lost, indeed, in a haze of vicarious pleasure. Catherine living on the Hawktoun Road, among professional folk and high-class tradespeople. Between them, they would make *Ardrishaig* into a home to be proud of. *She* would visit and help every day. Clamouring in her ear were the comments from the likes of Shambling Boots and Wrinkled Headscarf. "Lizzie Bathgate's girl—yes, she's bought a place outright on the Hawktoun Road. Of course, she married into money, you know."

"I want everything modern," said Catherine positively. She would be dependent on her mother for running up curtains and covering chairs, so would have to draw a fine line between appearing to heed parental advice and quietly achieving the effect she wanted.

In the days to come, she set up her home quickly and competently, feeling a quiet glow as each task was accomplished. Like her mother, she had always admired the tidy villas on the Hawktoun Road, with their solid front gates, barbered lawns and hedges and handsome oriel windows with their heavy curtains and flourishing castor oil plants. They spoke of tradition, stability, respectability, permanence and unchallengeable superiority over the *hoi polloi*. With Edward fighting in Europe, though she did not know quite where, but likely to be there for some unforeseeable time, she slipped into what she realized was an unforgivable kind of contented secure existence, life in a vacuum, where things were ordered to her will and she did not have to give into the necessity for suffering. When the agonizing feelings threatened to begin, she would tackle the decorating of another room, would worry about dyeing, matching, making over and making do. When all that was more or less accomplished, she arranged for extra pupils to come to her home for tuition in the evening, charging them higher rates because of the classier district. And so she was never really lonely. She was happy enough when she thought only of work.

She was surprised one evening to be visited by Christie-Ann on her own.

"Mother's got a sore throat. She thought she'd better stay in and treat it. She sent you the curtains she's finished for the kitchenette."

Christie-Ann suddenly had an awkward look, like a child about to seek a favour.

They hung the curtains there and then, after Catherine had smoothed out a few wrinkles with the iron, then Christie-Ann said with a slight nervous tremor of the mouth, "Catherine, I thought I'd be the best one to tell you. I'm seeing Colum Brodie."

She was looking at her sister's back, which instantly went rigid. Then Catherine slowly turned, her face changed from vivacity to a crumbling disbelief.

"You're what?"

"I'm seeing Colum. We're going out together. Someone else would tell you if I didn't."

"Well, you can't."

"What's to stop me?"

Catherine gave an involuntary step

forward towards her sister. "There can never be anything serious between you and him. You're deluding yourself."

"You think he still carried a torch for you? He told me just the other night you no longer mattered a thing to him. He's over you. And you have to get into your head you're married to somebody else and your loyalties are to him!"

Catherine sat down on one of the carefully covered, overstuffed armchairs. She was very pale and her teeth appeared to be chattering. "We've got to talk about this, quietly and sensibly. It isn't a question of who is over whom."

Christie-Ann sat down, too. They faced each other across the hearth.

"People can't help these things," said Christie-Ann, pleadingly. "It's just the way it's happened."

"Have you—does Mum know about this?"

"No. I haven't told her."

"Oh, Christie-Ann!" Catherine let her breath out on a long trembling sigh. "After what happened between him and me."

"I know. You had a baby and it died.

95

It was all a long time ago. You made your feelings clear when you didn't wait for him to come back from the war. He's not a plaster saint. He needs a flesh and blood woman to love him, not a ghost of a memory."

"And you do?"

"Love him?" Christie-Ann looked vulnerable and even younger than her years. "Oh, yes. I'm going to marry him, if I can."

Catherine put her hand to her mouth as if to stop anguish pouring out of it like ectoplasm and ran out of the room. Like someone in a silent movie, thought Christie-Ann, though without irony, and listened to her sister's footsteps go upstairs and then her bedroom door click shut. She did not know what to do next. She sat for a while, got up and twitched the hem of one recently hung curtain, took a sip of milk from the gauze-covered milk jug then eventually called up, "Catherine! I'm going home, then."

The bedroom door opened. Catherine's puffy face, dishevelled hair falling over it, appeared over the banisters.

"Ask him to come and see me."

"Why? There's nothing for you and him to talk about."

"Ask him. Please, Christie-Ann, do this one thing for me."

The girl in the hall twirled on her heel in an agony of indecision.

"All right. But you'll see. He loves me."

"You've snow on your collar." Catherine opened the door to Colum's ring and with an almost wifely, commonplace gesture brushed the offending flakes on to the vestibule floor. He stamped his feet on the mat and she went on in the same ordinary voice, though the inflection had risen slightly, "I have never known a winter like it."

"It's our chaps in the Ardennes I keep thinking about." He removed his coat and beat his arms together. "Bloody war goes on forever, doesn't it, just like the cold."

"Yes. Come in and get warm. Would you like some tea?"

He shook his head.

She sat down formally opposite him. He looked carefully round the freshly decorated lounge. It had pale green stippled walls, a green carpet on parquet tiles and glossy rexine chairs. On a shiny honey-coloured table by the window some white chrysanthemums stood stiffly to attention in a cream plaster vase. Everything was fresh and new and unused and but for the crackling fire and soft glow from a standard lamp might have appeared cold. Catherine, he thought, fitted in with the room. She was always so bandbox neat, so formal, yet her skin had a soft radiance, her movements were so delicate, there was no impression of hardness. He could feel his head begin to swim with conflicting emotions, with ungovernable sensations and yet he had come here determined to be calm. To impress her with his sang-froid and show himself he was over her. He had a sudden swift vision of Christie-Ann's anxious face and a warm surge of loyalty towards her surprised and heartened him.

"You're seeing Christie-Ann." Her hands, which had lain quietly in her lap, twisted in a quick spasm.

"Yes."

"Do you think it's a good idea?"

"I didn't have it as an 'idea'. It just happened."

"Well, Colum, it can't." She said it decisively, but the turbulence of some inner feeling brought her out of her chair to walk about the room.

He was about to respond when she held up her hand. "Listen. I have something to tell you. You know when we were having —having our affair? And when—the inevitable happened? And the parents—well, my mother mainly—decided that I should go away to my aunt's in Inveraray to have the baby? And you thought the baby died?"

She stood and watched the blood drain from his face. He could not ask the question, but she gave him the answer anyhow. "Well, he didn't." She let the bold statement lie for several seconds before she went on. "We told Christie-Ann what we told you and your parents, that it had been a still-birth. But he's called Struan and he lives with a second cousin near Inveraray. He's nearly three years old now, Colum."

"And do you see him?" He did not know where his voice came from. It did not sound like his.

"I don't. I won't. It was meant to be

put behind me. My cousin's childless. She loves him like her own. So I'm told."

"You did this to me?" He looked at her as though at some stranger. "Have you told him? The bottle-shouldered Englishman? Does he know?"

She shook her head. "I'll never tell him. You can tell him if you like."

"No! He'll not hear from me. Poor bugger."

"And Christie-Ann? Will we tell *her*?"

He did not answer her at once. Instead, lighting a cigarette, he paced up and down the room like an animal in a cage. At last he said, in a half-broken way, "Struan, you tell me . . . My son. *My* son! Catherine, how could you do this to me?"

She wept then, sitting huddled in one of the stiff chairs like a marionette whose strings have been severed. "I don't know."

"You must know!"

"I was frightened. About what people would say." She found a vestige of pride, of spirit, and cried, "You were away, don't forget. You had agreed I should go to my cousin's for my sake, as you put it. We were all trying to protect my name."

"And? And?" he urged.

"My mother started on me there. About how I would never be able to lift my head again. About sinking into poverty if I married you. About your family. I didn't know where to turn, Colum. I wanted us all to be together but there was this gulf and my mother's insistence on our self-respect. I was just beginning to earn decent money, to contribute to the house, to get established as a teacher. You know what it's like to be hard-up. And Catriona kept on and on about wanting to take the baby . . ."

He turned away as though he could no longer bear to look at her.

"You didn't need to marry him. Elkins."

"I know. But I did. I wish I never had."

"Leave him."

She said, almost indifferent now to pain, "I've been through all that. I cannot. He's done nothing."

"Well then," he said, furiously grinding out the cigarette, "I intend to marry Christie-Ann. She *cares* for *me*. She's a sight more independent than you'll ever be. And as for your—your monster of a mother, Christie-Ann has the strength of character you never had, to stand up to her. Break the ties, Catherine, or you'll never have a life. You hear me?"

"Don't you think I try?" she said, in a little voice. She gazed down at her hands in her lap, then asked:

"Do you agree to leave Struan where he is?"

"He's well cared for? Do they need money?"

She shook her head. "They need or want nothing."

"Then best leave it. You've finished us. I'll never be able to feel the same about you after this."

"Just as well," she said hardly. "Go to her, then. The wonderful Christie-Ann. My sister!" She stood up, arms akimbo and waited for him to leave. The looks they exchanged at the last were full of pain and anguish.

4

IN the years that followed her marriage, Christie-Ann never went deliberately to see her sister. If she called on Catherine, it was always because she "just happened to be passing". Catherine never visited Christie-Ann. She did not like going into the run-down council housing "scheme" because if she took the car children sat all over the bonnet and if she walked she got hard suspicious looks from slatterns gossiping at gates. She was a snob, Christie-Ann said. But there were other reasons, of course.

This morning, however, Christie-Ann had decided on waking that she would just happen to be passing her sister's home later in the day. She had no option. She would have to ask Catherine for money. She had resisted the notion with silent tears, with angry churning protest in her mind that had made her unable to eat a bite at breakfast. But it had to be done. There was no-one else to turn to and the children would go hungry if she did not solve her financial difficulties. It was no good that part of her mind still protested she would rather die than ask Catherine for help. Such histrionics solved nothing. Pride put nothing in the babes' mouth. And so she walked towards the Hawktoun Road, "just passing", Christie-Ann blurred the issue of her visit slightly in her thoughts. Catherine was lonely in that big house. Edward was often away on business. Certainly Catherine had the college, but she took every Wednesday off, ostensibly to catch up with household chores and shopping. Mainly she mooned around kitchen or garden, tidying what was already tidy, straightening what was already straight. Seeing the children might cheer her up.

"I don't want to go to my Aunt Catherine's," said Clare straight-forwardly. These days she challenged almost every decision that Christie-Ann made. She hung on grimly to the side of the push-chair wherein her sister, Lindsay, sat with a stoic air of co-operation, as Christie-Ann led the little caravan down Dounhead main street.

"Why?"

"Because she hangs on to her money."

"Where did you hear that?" A mad guilty mirth pervaded Christie-Ann's consciousness. At five Clare was already as sharp as a needle.

"From you. You told Daddy."

"Watch your mouth. Don't come out with things like that."

"I willn't," promised Clare.

"Aunt Cafferine," pronounced Lindsay from her push-chair, and evidently labouring under an access of strong emotion, as she twisted round red-faced to confront her parent, "she say don't touch the fowfs. That's what she say to me."

"It's flowers, not fowfs," shouted Clare. "What a baby you are, Lindsay."

"I not a baby." Christie-Ann aborted argument. She tweaked her elder child's arm and thrust the push-chair with Lindsay in it against the wind as they turned into Hawktoun Road. Had she and Catherine been like these two, she wondered. She didn't remember it like that, but her mother assured her they had argued all the time. Time's compression, of her own life and her sister's, seemed to make her and Colum's inability to provide largesse for their children all the more poignant.

And she was nothing like so good as her mother at making a little go a long way, maybe because she so resented the need for it. The coats the girls wore had been washed once too often; the baby's was matted and Clare's had several stains. Their shoes were scuffed and a size too small. Even their socks looked thin, all the body pulled out of them. I see they get food in their belly, she thought defensively. But she wanted nice things for them, things you could buy, not make down or make over. New and pretty things. It was a bloody irony she had the children but Catherine had the money.

She went round to the back door, knowing how fussy Catherine was about her steps and the push-chair in the polished hall. Her sister wore a smart dress and court shoes, as though ready to go out, but her greeting was cordial, if surprised. The children stepped warily, suspiciously, in the polished house, like scouts from an invading army wondering where it would be best to attack first.

Catherine divested Lindsay of her coat and took her on her knee. Christie-Ann noted that she was always more affectionate to the younger. Clare came and stood gravely by her mother's knee, like a figure in a studio photograph, her small face watchful.

"Would you like a parkin biscuit?" asked her aunt.

The children relaxed once they began to feel more at home. They played a game that cast Clare as hectoring school-mistress and Lindsay as long-suffering duffer of a pupil. There were only outbursts when the role of martyr grew too much for her and she played some quiet tangential game of her own till Clare toned down her bossiness.

"How's Edward?" asked Christie-Ann.

"Busy." There was a conclusive note to Catherine's voice.

"And Colum?"

"Skint," said Christie-Ann.

"So what's new?"

"I can't take any more of it. That's what's new. I'll have to leave Lindsay with his mother and get a job."

"That would be a pity. She'd let the child run wild."

Christie-Ann's face and voice were almost without expression.

"I was wondering, Catherine, if I could ask you for some money. To tide us over. I'm terribly short."

"How does Colum justify it? It's been like this since you married." Catherine put the question gently, knowing without looking, her sister's embarrassment.

"You know what he's like. He thought the advertising would pick up, but it hasn't. He has a big bill for paper. I don't know how he'll pay it."

"And they feed off him, the family, don't they, like vultures? Mum is right about the Brodies. They don't change."

"Colum can't say no to anybody."

"Then it's time *he* changed. What about the novel he was going to write?"

"Colum's just Colum, Catherine. These days he'd rather gamble."

"How much do you need?"

"Can you make it twenty?"

"I'll make it twenty-five."

"I'll pay you back."

"In your own time."

When Christie-Ann had gone, Catherine felt restless. She had not gone to the wedding of her sister and Colum Brodie. They had decided on a very quiet registry office ceremony, with only a friend on either side for witness. Afterwards there had been a period of estrangement but slowly she and Christie-Ann had rebuilt a kind of relationship, wary and formal, which did not include Colum. Now she felt one of her periodic bursts of yearning for him. Being married to Edward had not changed that.

The only thing was, she knew all the arguments for and against off by heart. The *con* list was much longer than the *pro*. The *pro* was nothing more than this desperate malaise of longing that reconstructed their brief time together, everything he had said to her, everything she had said to him, with an unsparing clarity of detail. Of course she should have nothing to do with him. He was married to Christie-Ann. He was the father of Clare and Lindsay. He should be nothing to her, a perfunctory adjunct to her real life, yet he was central to it. Her secret, central core, the image in front as she marched along life's road. There was nothing she could do about it. She couldn't talk about it to Edward. Or to Christie-Ann. The Catherine who went to college, who taught unwilling silly girls how to earn a livelihood, denied it. Mrs. Edward Elkins, respected in the local shops, looked up to by her neighbours, approved of by her mother, had no part in these secret rendezvous with memory. But the autonomous, unreconstructed, vital, instinctive, unreasoning Catherine took nourishment from the biggest emotional catharsis in her life—the year when she had been seventeen and given herself to Colum Brodie, heart, body and soul. No use saying she should retract all this. It was so. She had to live with it as best she could. At these times she was filled with a wild, creative energy. Sometimes she could expend it on the college, sometimes on the house but today she brooded about Colum's poverty and inability to make things go at the *Courier*. Giving Christie-Ann the money had been like giving it to Colum, but it was not enough. He needed more help, real help, the kind no-one else was in a position to give him.

She and Edward had separate bank accounts. So if she chose to go and see Colum today and offer to pay the newsprint bill, Edward need not know. Once she had thought of this supportive act, she could not leave it alone. She could feel warmth and a kind of happiness invade her whole being in a way it had not done for months.

She dressed in a warm, bronze-coloured coat with balloon sleeves and set an ocelot pillbox on top of her short, freshly-washed hair. There was a cravat to match the hat. She was pleased with her appearance. Somehow a recent haggardness had disappeared from her expression. She gazed in the hall mirror on her way out. She looked a little hectic. The lips upturned in a model's smile trembled back at her, just a little.

Colum sat behind his editor's desk with a pencil behind his ear. His shirt was crumpled and the sleeves were rolled up. There was a tiny hole in his maroon pullover. He looked startled, possibly even dismayed, as she walked in and half-rose as he said her name on a querying, half-incredulous note.

111

"Catherine!"

She closed the door carefully behind her.

"Hello, Colum." She held out a formal hand. "I've just had a visit from Christie-Ann and the kids. I thought I might as well say hello to you too."

"Hello," he replied, carefully. Then, because he could not help it, "It's wonderful to see you, Catherine. It's been a very long time."

"I know. I've decided to be grown-up about—things. Colum, I've come to see if there is anything I can do to give the business a lift. The college is doing well. Can I invest in the *Courier*?" She had not meant to put it quite like that, but the words came tumbling out. "I am good on the business side of things. Maybe I could help with the books." When he said nothing, merely looked embarrassed, she said, "Christie-Ann told me this morning there was a big newsprint bill outstanding. I'll clear that if you like. And we'll take it from there."

He placed his forehead in the heel of his hand, and remained so for a long second. Then, looking up, he said, emotionally,

"If anyone had told me this morning someone would walk in like this, with an answer to my prayers—"

"I don't know quite why I came," she said, equally emotional. "In a way it was like taking my life in my hands. Literally."

He came round the desk, lifted her up by her elbows and took her into his arms. He did not hug her to him, or attempt to kiss her. Just encircled her with his arms and looked down into her face.

"Aren't you happy?" he said simply, urgently.

"What's happy?"

He dropped his arms again and turned away to the window.

"Ah well, what indeed? I'm glad you see Christie-Ann and the kids. Whether it's practicable for you and me to meet—"

"I think it is. On this level, Colum, the business level. It would give me great pleasure to think I was helping you. And Christie-Ann for that matter."

"She might not take to the idea."

"Then shall we not tell her? Not for now, anyhow."

He gave her a guilty look.

"Something else to keep back from her? Does it strike you as fair?"

"You said a minute ago 'What's happy?' Now I'm saying 'What's fair?' I'll go away if you want me to, however."

"I could tell her you'd offered to help periodically with the books. That would explain matters if you're seen coming here."

"I'll be circumspect, I promise." She gazed at him, unconsciously imploring, then took her cheque book from her handbag and began to write. "What shall I make it out for? One hundred? Two?"

"Two-fifty. Christ, thanks." He drew down a tangled mass of papers from the top of a filing cabinet and handed them to her. "You can look through these if you like."

"These are your accounts?" she said, horrified.

"Bills. Demands. Mainly."

"But your advertisers? Your income—"

"One or two debts outstanding. I'm bad at chasing them up."

"I'll do it." Her face was alight with resolution. "Oh, I'm going to enjoy this. Say you can square it with Christie-Ann?"

"I think so. I'll try."

"Tell her I'm doing it from the purely practical angle. To help her and the children as well as you."

"Of course." His voice was warm and soft. "Jesus, I'm glad the thaw is on its way. It had to come from you, Catherine. You know that, don't you? Will Edward mind?"

"Edward's very busy." Her voice held the same note of unconscious warning as when Christie-Ann had mentioned her husband earlier in the day.

"That's not a proper answer."

"It's the one I choose to give."

She picked up the cheque, which he had not yet touched, waved it at him and then placed it in the centre of his desk. He took it up, looked at it then kissed it. Looking at it again, he said, "I've always liked your handwriting. Neat and pretty. Like its proponent."

She smiled at him without reserve. "What a daft word to use. Proponent." They sat in comfortable silence, not moving; as though, if they did, some kind of spell would be broken. Afterwards, she was always to think of the newspaper smell

—hot metal from the linotype, printer's ink. But at last she got up and said as though on an afterthought, "Get Christie-Ann to mend the hole in your jersey." As he stood close to her, she put a hand up, touched the back of his neck, ruffled his dark hair and added, "And you need a haircut, you do."

He caught her hand, kissed the palm. "Are you going, then?"

"I have to."

"Take care. I don't want any untoward winds blowing on you."

"There you go again. First proponent. Then untoward." Her look was the first to slide away. She walked quickly up the lobby and out of the rickety street door.

"Did you see your mother?" asked Edward. He did not usually catechize her but there was something cagey about her account of her day off that made him curious.

"Uh-huh." There, he hadn't imagined it. She did not meet his eyes. She was making griddle scones. "More coffee?"

"You know I never have a second cup. Was she in one of her moods, then?"

"No, not at all. Why do you ask?"

"You seem—preoccupied."

She smiled at him then, her wide, transforming smile that never failed to soften him. "My mother's moods are not my sole preoccupation, Edward. Not any more."

"What's the position with Christie-Ann?" Ever since her marriage to Colum, Lizzie Bathgate's younger daughter had had a continuously fraught relationship with her mother. Each time Christie-Ann visited Lizzie, she was left in no doubt about the sin she had committed. Colum was *persona non grata*. From week to week no-one knew whether Lizzie and Christie-Ann were on speaking terms. Long frosty silences on Lizzie's part were breached by strained, formal visits by Christie-Ann and the children. Visits Lizzie made it clear she only tolerated because in true Dounhead fashion she cared what the neighbours might say, not because she wanted to extend the hand of forgiveness or understanding.

"Same as ever. Mother says the children make her head ache. She thinks they need walloping."

He knew what she was thinking whenever Christie-Ann's children were mentioned. Like a wide, half-explored strip of territory between them lay the fact of their own childlessness. She seemed more and more reluctant these days to discuss it, but Edward was not fooled.

Catherine withdrew at the point of greatest hurt. Quiet and brooding, she showed her bewilderment only in her eyes.

He tried to open the subject up once again, as he did whenever he got the chance, obliquely. "I wonder what she'd think of one of ours."

Catherine threw down her napkin. "Don't," she said. "Don't. I know what you're up to."

"We have to talk about it, Catherine. It wouldn't hurt to get the doctor's advice."

"I don't want any doctor's advice. A child happens or it doesn't. If we are meant to have one, if it's God's will for us to have one, then we will. Leave well alone, Edward."

"You've never been as keen as I am. I wonder why that is."

"So it's going to be one of those 'I wonder why' evenings. Can't you be content with a wife who does everything in her power to make you happy? I cook you nice meals, we have a comfortable home and you have your garden, Edward. When you were away at the war you used to write that that was all you'd ask out of life. To be with me in our home."

He pushed his food to one side of his plate and looked at her, not consideringly, not contentiously, but with a long and lingering penetration that had a good deal of sadness in it. At last he said, "I am not getting at you, Catherine. I am not suggesting you have failed me in any way and I hope you don't think I've failed you. Our only failure is one of communication. If you don't tell me when you're unhappy, how can I help you?"

She said, "You keep analyzing and I just get tired of it."

"That suggests you are tired of me."

She did not reply to this. It was familiar ground. Instead, she cleared the table and washed up, while he changed into his gardening trousers and shoes and disappeared into the greenhouse at the bottom of the garden.

Later he emerged and began planting out young lettuce and cabbages. He was so meticulous and neat and the kitchen garden was always a pleasure to look at, flourishing, weed-free and well-planned. She felt resentment dribble away to be replaced by a kind of helpless, puzzled near-admiration. Always she waited for something stronger to invade her, but it never did.

She watched her husband work, his at first tentative manoeuvres turn to real absorption, and admitted she felt guilt. It was easy to take his adoration of her for granted, so easy to give him pleasure. His parents had been astonished that he was prepared to accept her line on where they lived, but his Englishness still stuck out like a sore thumb, he was never totally at ease with Dounhead locals, his attempts at coping with the local *patois* were still sometimes laughable. In the beginning he had said that anywhere she lived was good enough for him. And then his work had taken serious root in Glasgow, he and Alistair Cowie were a good partnership. What had started out with simple account-ancy had branched into import-export and their latest schemes were connected with self-service stores. She had laughed at first when he'd told her. "People will always want to be served," she'd said. But he'd maintained this was the way forward, that the day would eventually come when huge super-stores, selling everything, and with car parks to accommodate the customers, would be the accepted thing. When he talked about plans that caught his imagination she saw a different, younger Edward. She remembered now with a guilty twinge that there had been an important business meeting for him that day, with American interests hopeful of buying their way into the scene with something called computers using vacuum tubes.

Carefully she dried her hands, tidied her hair and walked down the garden path.

"How did the meeting go today? Sorry, I should have asked."

Something she had never seen in his expression, a hardness, a shutting out, hit her like a blow between the eyes. He looked directly at her and said curtly, "Well. It went well. Thank you for asking." And disappeared dismissively into the greenhouse.

"I want a two-column display ad for our

new term," said Catherine clearly. It was for the benefit of the sharp-eyed young assistant—you could hardly call him a reporter yet, as he was only fifteen, but it was what he aspired to—whom Colum had taken on and who was struggling manfully with an ancient typewriter in a corner of the office.

"Brian," said Colum, "I want you to ask Councillor Bell about the subsidence near the railway line. Leave that football report —you've been at it long enough."

"Yes, Mr. Brodie," said the boy. He picked up his notebook and pencil and left. They watched his Brylcreemed head recede before he came round his desk and touched her cheek lightly with his lips.

"You shouldn't do that," she demurred.

"What? Not kiss my sister-in-law?"

"No. Not ever."

"Does it matter so much to you? Every breath you take matters to me."

"Colum—the ad. We've extended, you know. Room for twelve more."

"Catherine, I think I'm going mad."

"So how much would the ad cost?"

"Nothing. Nothing. To you, nothing."

"How can you say that? Sit down,

Colum, please, I want to talk to you very seriously. You have to take yourself in hand. You must stop giving people you like space in your paper for nothing and that includes me—"

"I don't *like* you. How dare you use a word like *like*. I think about you every waking moment. I'm like a drunk man, not responsible for his actions. Christ, Catherine, nothing's changed. You have to come away with me—"

He sat down at her bidding and now she found herself standing close beside him with her arms wrapped round his neck while his encircled her waist. She stood perfectly still and he remained, too, without moving.

"I love you," she said, gabbling. "I haven't been alive for years and the minute you touch me—"

"Christ, tears," he said, wiping hers from off his own face. She fell face down, on to him, unable to bear the weight of her own passion. He held her and dragged her to the door, where he turned the lock. He led her into the little anteroom where a green blind was drawn at the tiny window and they kissed like two people dependent on it for their very existence. She said his name over and over again, like a mantra and he did the unbuttoning when the need for it was heedlessly apparent. Even after the climax of their love-making they could not bear to move apart. He had to touch her face and kiss her lips and she looked as though she had no power in her limbs apart from him.

She had arranged to meet Mary Mackinnon at the college at three-thirty. Normally she kept away from the college on her day off, feeling that Mary enjoyed her one-day stint of being totally in charge. It had worked well, the partnership, over the years. Ostensibly this meeting was to discuss next year's syllabus, but she had a feeling there was something else Mary wanted to talk about.

She walked along Dounhead Main Street trying to assume her usual air of rather formal reserve, yet feeling that everything about her was altering, that her body, her facial planes, were melting, reconstructing in a seamless way into a totally different being. It was joyful and at the same time frightening and she did not know whether she could achieve control of the new phenomenon.

She went into Beveridge the baker's and ordered a sponge cake with cream decorated with tangerine segments, just because she liked the look of it. While there she conducted an unusually animated discussion about the weather with Miss Anderson, the faintly astonished manageress, with whom relations had been frosty ever since the rigours of bread rationing.

"You look as though you've had a nice morning," said Mary. She had the college's silver tea-service at the ready and on an impulse Catherine opened the cakebox and cut them each a section of cake.

"Not like you to indulge," said Mary, wiping cream from her fingers. "What is it? Somebody's birthday?"

Catherine shook her head, smiling. "Not really." Mary held her questioning look, but seeing she would get no further, went on: "I've got something to tell you, so I might as well come out with it. I'm going to America."

"Why?"

"I've been writing to a GI I knew in the war and he wants me to go out and marry him."

"You sly puss! You never let on."

"I never thought it would come to anything," Mary admitted. She had broad cheekbones, a broad behind and a fresh-faced country prettiness. "But Calvin's mother has died and it puts a new construction on things. He wants a woman on the farm."

Catherine kissed Mary on the cheek, her mind whirling with the implications of this new development.

Later, after she'd heard a full account of the postal romance, she said, "Does this mean I buy you out, then?"

Mary nodded. "You can run this place without me. It's your presence that dominates anyhow, Catherine. You're the presiding genius." She looked up at her friend and partner with a kind of embarrassed affection. "You're becoming quite a figurehead in the town. I can see you standing for the council next. I can never see you moving away from here, Catherine. I've always had a restless nature

126

but you, you're different. You like calm and order and tradition. Am I right?"

"I don't know."

"There's a letter in this morning, asking you to be examiner for the area in shorthand and typing. And another asking you to give a talk to the Rechabites—"

"Maybe I'm not what I seem to be, altogether," she said shortly.

"You, Catherine?" Mary threw back her dark curls and laughed. "You're everything good and Scottish and reliable. Don't backtrack on me now."

5

THEY met every day for a week, twice in the *Courier* office, twice in the dark in woods near Dounhead, once in a Glasgow tearoom, in Hawktoun at the cinema. Their love was like a sickness they knew they had no hope of recovering from: what they had to do was find ways of living with it and with those around them. But they had the curious sensation sometimes that only they existed and all else were ghosts and spirits.

They threatened each other with calamity if the one addressed withdrew love: they promised that what they felt then would last into eternity. Every touch and look unleashed passion, every looking away induced regret that grew into unassuagable sorrow. Everything about the other became precious, the way hair grew, the line of a cheek, the cut of a coat, the cracks or the dust on a pair of shoes. Names were talismans, endearments were those that had never been used before.

Their happiness had a lunacy to it, their behaviour towards each other childish to the point of infantile and noble to the point of sacrifice. He would go away, he said, if she asked him to; he would die if he did. She would forget she had ever seen him; she would change her religion and wall herself up in a nunnery.

On the seventh day she told him she could not go on living with her husband. She would have to find some way of separating from him that did not involve telling him about Colum. She would simply tell him their marriage had not worked and that if he wanted children he should divorce her and find someone else.

"You can't leave Christie-Ann," she said. He could not really argue with her. It was not so much Christie-Ann as the children. They thought of Clare and Lindsay, with their little wrists the span of a thumb and their skin as soft as rose petals and their milk-white baby teeth and their trust in those who loved them and some kind of sanity permeated the passion, like cream over scalding coffee.

"You're being silly," said Edward

patiently. "You're worried about Mary going and about running the college on your own. I say to you, give it up and let's go and live somewhere else. Get away from Dounhead."

"You'd like that," she said furiously. "You'd like to take me away from my roots and everything I've fought so hard to establish. The college is mine, more mine than it ever was Mary's, and I'll never give it up. It's my security, my independence—"

"You don't have to talk like that," he said bruisedly, "as though I've never supported you. Anything I have is yours—"

She brushed him away with a devastating gesture. "I can do without your support. I don't need anybody."

He came over and put his arms about her, pinioning hers down by her side. They looked out of the windows and down on the rain-soaked garden of the house in Hawktoun Road. A starling and two sparrows fluttered in and out of a puddle in the middle of the path.

She sagged and said wearily but determinedly, "I think we should separate. I'm tired of you going on about my child-lessness—"

"All I say is, let's find out why."

"And I say no."

"And I say you are being un-reasonable."

"Then my answer is: leave me. Leave me if you think I am so unreasonable."

He began to walk about the room. Now that there was more choice in the shops, it was furnished with great comfort and some style. Occasionally he brought business contacts home for a meal, but recently Catherine had resisted that, too. His life was becoming more and more untenable here as Catherine sought daily grounds for confrontation.

He had hoped that with the passage of time he would be able to understand his wife better. It had gone the other way. She had become more and more of an enigma to him. He could not get close to her mentally; and physically, when he coaxed and wheedled her to turn to him in bed, he might as well have slept with a rag doll. Sometimes she wept uncontrollably into his shoulder; at other times she despatched his urges with a cold efficiency that left him in the depths of despair.

His mother had warned him about marrying out of his class. And about women being like their mothers. Was hard, joyless, parochial, censorious Lizzie Bathgate, with her obsessional ways and her strictures against life and her neighbours, coming out in Catherine? Would Catherine become hard, rigid, resistant to all change? He did not want to face this possibility. He still loved his wife, who was unchanged in looks since the day they'd met. Pretty, shapely, with a flair for wearing subtle, attractive clothes, for moving with an unconscious dainty grace. Clever, quick, organized, too—he could not bear sloppy women.

But hope deferred did make the heart sick. The poet wasn't wrong. He could feel frustration and anger curdle in him from the moment he woke, so that everything he did and touched was somehow out of kilter all day long. He—they—couldn't go on like this. He thought of seeing a doctor, even a psychiatrist; he had tried putting the idea up to Catherine. Maybe they should seek advice from a marriage specialist, he'd suggested. But he knew the answer wasn't in consulting anybody. It lay in him and in a certain blurry softness in his make-up that came from his sheltered upbringing.

"Catherine," he began again hopelessly, then could say no more. His rolled-up shirt sleeves had become unrolled, so that the cuffs flapped, but he paid no heed. He looked curiously dishevelled, like a man who has been taken apart in a bout of fisticuffs. For a moment she looked at him with something like pity, something like horror, certainly not with love and then she stopped in her tracks and waited. "Yes," she queried.

"It is over, then?" He put the question softly.

She nodded without hesitation and managed a kind of compassion at the last. "Yes, I'm afraid it is."

"Will you want me to go straight away?"

"Can you find somewhere? What about Glasgow?"

"Alistair wants me to go to America for three months, on a computer course. I think it would be a good idea. Shall we regard it as a trial separation? Then when I come back—"

"I'm sorry," she said stiffly. "But haven't you known for a long time that it would not work out?"

"It could have done."

"Please," she said. "Don't start. I really cannot bear it."

"I have this pain here," said Lizzie Bathgate, "and I get awfu' tired at times."

"You should see the doctor, Mother. Would you like me to ask him to call in?"

Lizzie gave her short, scornful laugh. "Doctors! They kill more than they cure. Naw, naw, I'll get some Phosperine. That does the trick."

"Well, if you're sure. You don't have to wash down the kitchen walls once a week, you know. You could send your sheets to the laundry. It's not as though you can't afford it."

"I'll do it my way." Lizzie gave indication that the subject was closed, but she sat back gratefully in her chair and let Catherine set the table and make the tea. Catherine scattered the haddock with breadcrumbs, fried it carefully, made

134

toast. As they began to eat, she said, "Well, the college is mine. Give me a couple of years and I'll buy the house for you, Mother. You wouldn't rather have a flat? It would be easier to keep clean."

"Naw, naw. I started my married life here and I'll finish it here." Lizzie got up and fished about in the long, shallow drawer of the kitchen dresser. "All your dad's bits of things are here. His medals—" she brought forth her husband's two medals from the First World War—"and his diary, wi' the instructions on how to set up his machine gun. I never bothered wi' such things when I was younger. Noo I've got the time—" she left the sentence unfinished and abruptly sat down again.

Catherine stared at her parent. This was as near to sentiment as she had ever heard her get. When they were growing up, she and Christie-Ann had urged their mother many times to tell them about their father, but she had always brushed them off with some harsh rejoinder—"Him! He couldnae keep a sparrow!" or "The wastrel! It was his bookie he was wed to, no' me."

What did it mean? That Lizzie was

permitting herself the luxury of feelings for the first time in her life? It made Catherine uneasy, almost as though she intruded on some long-ago private grief. She felt something well up in her that was so strange and new she could scarcely identify it; for so long, there had been resentment and hatred in her heart because her mother had been the chief architect of the parting from Colum and the baby. But underneath *before* the hatred, was the little girl who depended on that tired, stringy figure for any benison, any acceptance, any security there was in the difficult world. How she had tried to please! How she had looked for softness! How she had wanted—there was no other word for it— love.

But there hadn't been much of it about for her mother, she realized. Her mother's childhood had been unconscionably hard, her widowhood precipitate. And now she seemed to be putting out feelers, looking maybe for some tenderness from her elder daughter. Catherine searched but did not know if she could find it. Bewildered, she said with more acerbity that she intended, but reiterating the philosophy that Lizzie herself had dished out, "Well, it doesn't do to get too introspective. 'Sufficient unto the day is the evil thereof'."

"You should never have left your man." It was as though, picking over the fish for bones, Lizzie looked for wounds to poke. "He was a good man, Edward Elkins. Good from the start and good at the finish."

"No good for me," said Catherine summarily.

"What went wrong?" asked Lizzie, with unwonted concern. "He took you to the shows—the theatre, I mean—he took you to the opera. He said to me, 'Mother,' he said, 'I'm filling in the gaps. The sensibility is there, only the education is missing.' He would have gone to the end of the world for you, Catherine. I'll never understand it."

"No?" said Catherine. "Well, why worry? We were never much into understanding each other, Mother. Like when you made me give away my baby. There were times—" Catherine rose and took her fish-plate into the scullery, running it noisily under the tap. When she came back, she sat down carefully and said in

137

a contained voice, "Don't let's upset each other. We'll get along fine if we keep off certain areas. I want to see you taking things easier, Mother. What about getting a television set? You like mine. You like Macdonald Hobley, don't you? It would be good company for you."

"Idle rubbish!" said Lizzie, dismissively, but after a few moments, when she had finished off her tea, she stirred restlessly and said, "Maybe I'll give it a try."

It was a question of who came to their senses first. Maybe the upset caused at the college by Mary's departure was a blessing in disguise, because the work, the attention she had to pay to detail, took Catherine's mind off her emotional troubles. And when she could allow herself time to think about herself and Colum, she was filled with a kind of sick, denying dismay that they could have done what they did. Had they really made love every day that first week, like two demented teenagers? Had she really despatched her husband as callously as it now seemed? Had they lied and plotted and deceived all around them? Had she done this,

Catherine Bathgate, who walked so proudly down the street each morning and expected, nay demanded, the respect of pupils, neighbour, family, as of right?

And of course, above all, there was Christie-Ann. She found it almost impossible to define her feelings towards her. From the moment Christie-Ann had made clear her determination to marry Colum, she had hated her. There had been times she knew she could not face her sister or she would say or do something that would devastate the relationship forever.

She had felt little or no compassion at first when things had gone wrong for Colum and Christie-Ann—the struggle with the paper, two difficult births, the children going from one childhood ailment to another. Perhaps part of her had even rejoiced. Only when Christie-Ann had become paler, more defeated, the archetypal young Dounhead mother dragged down by poor food and too little rest, had she found it in her heart to try and relate to her once again, to be the elder sister, the aunt, the mentor. She had not been able to shut out the children. In their innocence they ruthlessly broke down barriers and ignored snubs.

And when Christie-Ann had come to her for help she had found a huge willingness to do all she could. It had been like a coming in from the cold and because Colum was indirectly involved even then, like a great warming fire. She had ignored all the danger signals until it was too late. Helping Christie-Ann had turned into deceiving Christie-Ann, stealing her husband, behaviour unpardonable by any recognized canons of decency.

And she saw now, it was no good pleading they had not been able to help themselves. She should not have allowed herself to be alone with Colum; she should never have put temptation in their way. What she felt now was worse than any previous pain. It was as though she were split open and every nerve ending exposed to regret, humiliation, despair. If it killed them, it would have to stop. (And if they stopped, would it kill them? It could not be helped.)

She made him come to see her at home, late at night, leaving the car a distance away, slipping in the back door like a cat in the dark. And they sat talking, no reserves, no holds barred, about what was feasible, for as long as was necessary.

They both wept, in the end it was almost matter-of-fact, and touched each other's hands, dried each other's tears. They decreed that they had come to the end of love-making, that henceforward they would only meet when third parties were present. They began, even, to think hopefully that their passion had been a storm which had blown itself out, leaving them adult, scourged and in control.

She would keep her interest in the paper, because that was in the interest of Christie-Ann and the children, too. And would she try again with Edward? He wanted to know. He did not like to think of her living alone in the big house in Hawktoun Road. She shook her head, but he could see in her eyes she was afraid of the loneliness he specified and for a moment he was riven with jealousy, the good all the talking had done was almost undone.

"Pray, Colum," she said, when she let him go. "It's all we've got left to us."

"No, not all." He shook his head.

Because they had talked about Struan, their son, during the brief period of their *liaison dangereuse*. He held her then, till the pain drained out of her. She managed a smile as she said, "At least he's happy. Out of all this."

She began to dictate to the class from yesterday's paper. "Everest, conquered at last thanks to the stubborn bravery of Edmund Hillary and the faithful persistence of Sherpa Tensing . . ." but her thoughts were not with the girls labouring over their shorthand notebooks. Edward had telephoned her from Southampton yesterday, to say he had docked, that he was coming to see her as soon as he got back to Glasgow. He had sounded cheerful, upbeat and had ignored the demurring note she knew was in her voice. "New York was wonderful," he said. "I've got such a lot to tell you." She looked around at her girls, as though to reassure herself all this existed: the college, the desks, the books, the scheduling of classes. The chatter and the clatter. The industrious silences. The smell of perfumes and the sweat of effort. Her eyes lighted on this girl who turned in a perfect shorthand note and that one whose work was all over the place, who would never get herself together. She was shaken with affection for them, even the dimmest.

There was no welcome in her for him. These days she felt used-up, thin, cold. She wore her warmest clothes, but she still felt cold. Sometimes, in private she wept, but there was no luxury in the tears, they were almost spent, squeezed out of her, leaving her red-lidded, sore-nosed.

When she got home, however, she found herself tidying the house in a more purposeful way. She had found some *Cries of London* prints for the lounge and thought fleetingly that would please him. They had always been able to discuss books, painting, what was in the newspapers. She thought: I'll ask him what inflation means; I'll ask him about Britain exploding the Bomb in Australia. And then she drew back. She was thinking like a wife and they had said finish to all that. She would have to match her opinions against somebody else, but it was true that there was no-one else so well-informed, who read between the lines of the popular Press with such scrupulous care. He had often irritated her with his talk of "trained minds", but she knew now what he meant. She disliked sloppy generalizations and made herself look beyond popular assumptions. He had taught her that . . . hadn't he?

Poor Edward! What had he done to deserve her? She thought that if he suggested they live together again, she would have to tell him about Colum, yet something in her resisted this notion with all her might. There was no telling what he might do . . . He was not a man given to venting anger in a physical way, but he could be cold, even vindictive if pushed far enough and . . . She realized she didn't really know how Edward might react. He might kill himself. Or her. She had done enough harm. She could at least protect him from this.

But she did not know how much courage she had, or how much resolution.

He had gone a little grey at the temples. It was the first thing she noticed and she felt it was unfair, a blackmail. His features seemed more set, a little waxen and you would not exactly call him a *young* man, any more, although once he spoke his manner was animated enough and warmed the pale skin, the careful, hesitant frame.

He had brought her presents from Macy's, a Paisley blouse, a handbag and some costume jewellery. She had cooked roast beef and Yorkshire pudding and pressed a second helping of trifle on him. After the meal they remained at the table, elbows resting, and he said, "There was no point putting off seeing you, Catherine. I want us to try again. I'll plead if need be."

The bluish lids came up and she gazed at him broodingly. Before she could reply he was into a racing monologue: "I took Herman Coutts into my confidence—you know, my oppo in New York. He and his wife Etta were so warm and easy to talk to and they said there's every chance we'll still conceive, they were married five years before the miracle happened, now they have three, all we need to do is take steps like watching what time of the month you ovulate, it's quite easy to find out—do you ever get stomach pains halfway through the menstrual cycle, Etta says?—if you do, that means there's an egg and there's little things we can do like a cushion under you and eating certain things, I've got a diet sheet. Why do you look like that? Oh, Christ, I'm so clumsy, look forget it, all I want is for us to be together because you're still the girl for me. I'm a one-woman man, that's all. Catherine?"

"What if I am not a one-man woman?" Should she quietly finish him off? She could not do it.

"You mean you've met someone else?"

She shook her head quickly. "Not really. But it's silly to talk like that. We can all love more than one person in a lifetime, I'm sure of that. At least, I hope so."

"You're entitled to your opinion. All I'm saying is what I am. What I feel. How can you think of us giving up all this—" he waved a hand round the room—"when we put it together, you and I? Shall we have a dog, Catherine? We could pay someone to exercise it during the day. Shall we have a boat to sail on the Clyde?"

She was heeling tears away from her eyes and he came quickly round the table

146

and gave her a clean handkerchief from his pocket. His light, warm, dry hand rested on the nape of her neck. Custom, affection were there, but she bowed her head under the weight of her secret knowledge. She could not feel shame, never shame, it was never part of what she felt towards Colum, but there might have been regret and there was certainly sadness. She gave a great sigh, while his dark eyes, the eyes of a bright, intelligent schoolboy, never left her face.

"I don't think much will change," she whispered. "But if you want to, we'll try to go on. Don't—" she hesitated, knowing there was no way to put the next words without offence—"don't make too much of it. Of me. Don't expect too much. In any way."

He drew back. "It'll work out. It was good for me to be able to stand back from us for a month or two. I see a lot of things more clearly now. Is there more coffee?"

"You are looking very elegant, Mrs. Elkins, if I may say so." Alistair Cowie, his broad, honest face under its ridges of wavy hair smiling down affectionately at her, guided her into the front row of the stalls at the Theatre Royal in Glasgow. Behind him his wife Joyce, in a taffeta frock, chatted brightly to Edward in her somewhat affected Bearsden accent. They settled down expectantly, Joyce opened a large box of chocolates and passed them round and the handsome curtains rose on the opera *Cavalleria Rusticana* with a thrilling surge of Mascagni's music from the orchestra.

"Happy?" Edward took hold of his wife's hand in the dark and smiled at her. She had not missed the note of pleading. It said all he needed now was her compliance: they were here with his partner and his wife listening to the form of music he loved better than any other. The meal beforehand had been well-chosen and well-cooked. *All very civilized.* It was Edward's favourite phrase. She would not spoil it for him. She smiled and nodded, but in a moment withdrew her hand and concentrated on what was happening on the stage.

She had not been greatly attracted by opera in the past. Very often the noise, as she called it, gave her a headache. But this one was different. The music seemed to be seeking her out, to be moving through her very being, to be taking over her limbs. She was transfixed, transformed and begrudged even the interval and its noisy crush for drinks. The story, of course, was of a young soldier who has deserted his sweetheart to go in search of his former lover, now married to someone else and who is killed by the lover's husband in the tragic duel as the opera reaches its magnificent end.

She did not know she wept till Edward put out a hand and touched her. When they stumbled out towards their respective cars she could only manage a subdued "Good-night" to the other couple.

"Why were you so moved?" Edward asked, intrigued by her reaction.

"I don't know," she lied. In bed she gave herself up to him as though she gave herself up to her grief. She kept hearing the tragic arias in her mind, equating herself with Lola, the lover, and Santuzza with Christie-Ann. Above all, equating Colum with Turiddu, the soldier and Edward with the wronged husband. She had perceived something about the nature and profundity of human love, how it could be retained, in the very act of renunciation. Edward thought he detected a new tenderness, a new giving. "My darling girl," he said, his voice shaking. "Thank you for that. Thank you for tonight."

Catherine picked up the telephone some two months later and dialled the *Courier* number. "Is that Colum? Are you on your own?"

His half-alarmed voice sounded down the wire. "Catherine? Is something the matter?"

There was a long pause till at length she said, "It depends on what you mean."

"Catherine." He was genuinely alarmed now. "Tell me. What is it?"

"I have just been to the doctor and he's confirmed I'm pregnant."

He let out a gasping sigh of relief, which mixed with bittersweet concern in his next words. "Thank God. I thought—never mind what I thought."

"I wish it could have been yours."

He could not reply. She heard only the

150

rustle and crackle of the telephone line. "Colum? Are you there?"

"Darling, don't say those things."

"I do. I wish it could have been yours."

"Aren't you pleased? Is it something that *I'm* pleased, for you. I can see you with a child, Catherine."

"How are the family?" She asked it bleakly.

"The kids are fine. Christie-Ann's talking about getting a job. She says she's serious. Maybe it could help."

"Help what?"

"Help us all."

"God help us, Colum. God help us all."

6

THE sun radiated with a pale golden sheen into the nursery of the Maternity Hospital at Hawktoun. Five minutes ago all the occupants had been sleeping, or at least dozing and it had looked curiously, sentimentally, like an anteroom to the world. Then one or two had set up a wailing and now the whole place reverberated to hungry desperate cries. The nurses hastened in and out, taking the infants to their mothers in the wards to be fed. Soon all had been accommodated save one. The nurse picked up the little girl in the pink shawl and gave her a quick hug. "Whose mummy doesn't want her, then?" she murmured. "Come on, my lovely, you won't go without." And then she took her into a side ward and fed her from a bottle.

Edward had been waiting to see the consultant before he saw Catherine and his daughter. The man, like a large scrubbed pink elf, motioned him into a seat. Carefully the consultant sifted through his notes.

"Mr. Elkins? Yes . . . h'mm . . . three weeks now since the birth of your her-hum daughter. She's doing splendidly now. Quite splendidly."

"But my wife?" Edward tried, unsuccessfully, to stop his hands from twisting.

"Well, now, post-natal depression can take women in different ways. Mostly, it amounts to just a day or two of feeling a bit weepy. Natural, considering the upheaval a baby means. But occasionally it can be a bit more ah-hum intractable—"

"Why won't she see the baby?"

"We shall try to find out. You are taking her out for the day? Splendid. It may be just the tonic she needs."

"But I'm desperately worried—"

"Give her time." For the first time the consultant's bland blue gaze met his, then looked away.

"If only I understood more."

"We are beginning to think there could be hormonal factors, but—there is a her-hum psychological factor also. If she wants to talk, let her talk. It will sort itself out. Generally does."

153

Edward felt an unjustifiable fury towards the man and his complacency as he walked towards Ward 7B after seeing the baby. Catherine was sitting neatly on her made-up bed and gave him a tight little smile. He took her arm as they walked down the corridor together and out towards the car.

"Where to, madam?" He essayed a jocularity he did not feel.

"Wherever you like."

"I thought the Trossachs, then. Since the sun is shining." When she said nothing, he let in the gears. Presently she said, "Anywhere is better than that place."

He had made some egg sandwiches and filled a flask with coffee and they sat by the lochside in the chilly, silvery sun. He thought perhaps she would talk about the baby if first he made a fuss of her, thinking in his desperation that there might be some obscure, immature jealousy in her for the bursting satisfaction he had felt about his first-born.

But what she talked about was the college. How she could not wait to get back. How she thought they might eventually move to a tailor-made building nearer Glasgow.

"What about Jasmine Elizabeth?" he asked quietly.

"Oh, we'll have to have a nanny."

He bit back the angry words that wanted to come and instead said carefully, "We've never talked about that."

"No problem," she said, almost jauntily. "I don't want to get immersed in all that. You know, feeding and changing. Ughh!"

"But—"

"I think I want to get back now. I get tired very easily."

Kelsey, the clinical psychologist was young and pale with intense dark eyes and a tendency to let his hair grow long. She saw him twice a week and had done for several months. At home, the baby Jasmine was looked after by Isobel Lockhart, a serious, lanky girl from a village between Dounhead and Hawktoun.

What she had to do was relax and talk about whatever came into her head. There had been tears. Silences. Today she said to him with a note of challenge, "You think I'm cold towards the baby, don't you?"

"What I think doesn't matter. What do you think?"

"I am not naturally demonstrative. I hold back."

"Why do you think that is?"

Silence.

"You have told me how hard it was for your mother to show you affection. Do you think that might have something to do with it?"

"Everything, I suppose."

Silence, and then tears. Patiently, he handed her the clean hankie he kept in his top pocket for just such a purpose. "I've forgotten mine," she said, "again."

"It is all right."

"You could never do anything to please her. The hems you sewed were never straight enough. The cakes you baked were never light enough."

"Do you think she may have had an overbearing parent? One who demanded impossible standards from her?"

"Oh, yes."

"So in a way, she was unconsciously

156

passing on the burdens that had been laid on her."

"It's no good making excuses for her. There were other things she did."

"What things?"

But she was weeping again, turning her head away from him. In a few moments she got up and said she had had enough for one day. He helped her into her coat.

"This dream you had." Kelsey looked as though he had not slept too well himself. Did people go in for this kind of thing because they, too, had disturbed psyches? He had assured her often enough she was not alone in her kind of suffering.

"Yes?"

"The kitten was down a well. And you could not reach it. And then you thought it changed and was a baby."

"Yes."

"What baby?"

"I don't know."

"Could it have been your little girl? Could it have been Jasmine?"

"No. Another baby."

"*Another* baby?"

"Str-uan." The name came out in a long low wail. She reached up and grasped the cheap stuff of his jacket arm. Blindly she sought for his hand and held on to it. "Stru-an. The one she took away from me . . ."

He held her hand till the storm blew itself out. He offered her a drink of water. "You asked for him at the time of Jasmine's birth."

"I did? I don't remember."

He nodded down at her gravely. "How can I talk to you like this?" she asked. "How can people be as close and yet be—strangers? It's a kind of love. Isn't it?"

He nodded. "Kind of. When did you have Struan?"

"A long time ago. 'That was in another country and besides the wench is dead'."

"No. She is here. In this very room."

"I don't want to talk about the father."

"That's all right."

"But I loved him."

He looked down at her compassionately. "Yes."

"And I wanted the baby . . . ever since."

"I think we should have a holiday. Just the three of us."

Edward's head came up from his *Glasgow Herald* with a start. Was he hearing right? In the days and months since Jasmine's birth he had learned to tread so warily with Catherine, to be prepared for her moody withdrawals, her tensions, even her tears. But since the baby had passed her first birthday he thought he had detected a change in his wife. She took the baby over from Isobel more often, there was evidence of a stronger bonding between Jasmine and her mother and a general lightening of the atmosphere in the house in Hawktoun Road. He had scarcely dared to hope that Catherine was coming out of her post-natal depression. The idea of a holiday had been something he too had been toying with, but had been afraid to broach because Catherine had been so endlessly busy at the college. Endlessly and fussily, as though her life depended on it.

He said carefully, "Without Isobel?"

"Oh, certainly. I can manage my own daughter, for a couple of weeks." Catherine held the baby under her arms and encouraged her to take tip-toeing, half-dancing steps forward.

"You feel—you can cope?"

"I *am* better," she said fretfully. "I don't get so dreadfully tired. And besides you would be there."

"Fine. Right. Where shall we go?"

"I thought Arran. Brodick." She took the baby on to her knee. "You'd like that, wouldn't you, sweetheart? Lots of nice sand to play on. We'll get you a bucket and spade."

The baby had two teeth up top and two at the bottom. She gave a great Bugs Bunny grin and caught a handful of her mother's hair in a tight and painful grasp, refusing to let go. Edward felt it was his own innards that were being twisted. There were some states that were called happiness that were too complex for that: that twisted your feelings as unmercifully as Jasmine twisted her mother's hair.

"That's great," he said inadequately. "Let's do it."

There had been no holidays for four years because it had always been too difficult to synchronize their breaks. Now it seemed to him Catherine did nothing but spend and pack. There were new slacks and shirts for him, dresses for her and the

160

baby. She wanted everything organized and carefully thought out. "I hope nothing goes wrong," she said several times. "Why should it?" he responded. "Oh, you never know." She was a little strung-up, he thought, but determined.

On the morning they set off to catch the ferry he thought the day would remain in his memory as a highlight of his whole life. She was beautifully crisp and smart in a pleated blue dress, her figure fully restored after childbirth, her hair cut short and slightly back-combed on the crown in the fashion of the moment.

To see her pick up and carry the crowing, happy baby no-one would ever guess at the months of rejection, worry and depression she had been through. He felt she would always be more valuable to him because of her vulnerability, just as his child would always be precious because they had waited so long for her. And now he had both his women, they were together, a family, he could not think of a single item in the whole universe necessary to perfect his pleasure.

The weather decided to play along with them. Sunny day followed sunny day and they came out from large breakfasts in their hotel to sunbathing, rowing, fishing, walking, companionable afternoons lazily chatting to people from the hotel or licking ice-creams over well thumbed paperbacks.

"There's something I want to talk to you about," she said, one evening during the second week when Jasmine had been put to bed and they sat over long drinks in the hotel lounge. She smiled at him nervously.

"Oh? What is it?" He hoped it might be a proposition to stay on a few days more.

"It's important," she said. Her eyes were suddenly big and dark in her face and her tan seemed to have paled a little.

"How important? It won't spoil my drink, will it?" he joked. The baby had been a bit fractious that afternoon and the drink had been one he'd looked forward to with a singular keenness.

"It concerns us. Or more particularly me." She looked round to make sure they still had the lounge to themselves. Out on the lawn and beach the long shadows grew longer.

"I talked it out with Kelsey during my therapy with him. He thought perhaps I shouldn't tell you. I felt perhaps I should. Get it all out in the open and then there might be more genuine hope for all of us."

He looked at her in alarm. He hoped she wasn't going to be difficult and neurotic now, in the middle of their idyllic holiday. Strangely, the content of what she might say did not worry him. They'd covered a lot of emotional ground over the past months, with Kelsey's help and he supposed it might be some new insight into a childhood trauma, another episode in the embattled area that was his wife's relationship with her mother.

"Well?" he challenged.

"It is going to be very hard for me to tell you." She took a sip of her drink to moisten lips that had gone strangely parched. "I—I don't know if I can."

"Catherine!" he protested. "If it's something painful, can't it wait? Do you want to spoil the evening?"

She had been sitting tensely forward in her chair. Now she subsided and looked moodily out of the window for a long spell. Her head jerked about as though in response to the intensity of her feelings. At last she broke out, "No, it has to be done. Here goes. It's about me, when I was seventeen. I had an affair with Colum —yes, my sister's husband as of now, *that* Colum, and we had a baby, a baby I pretended had died but who lived and is now a boy of nearly fourteen."

Her breast heaved and she put a hand up to it as though to still the rapid beating of her heart. When he managed to look at her, her face looked set but she was totally dry-eyed.

He could say nothing as two people, a couple who had only recently arrived, had drifted into the lounge and were looking hesitantly at them as though they might settle near them for a chat. He gave them a brief, dismissive nod and half-turned away from them, so that slightly miffed, they looked momentarily through the window and then announced in loud voices they were going for a stroll.

She was saying now, in a hard, low, defensive way, "I never thought I could tell you, Edward, because you put me on such a pedestal. I tried to forget it myself. The boy is well looked after by a cousin of mine. But Kelsey made me see you've got to face up to the truths about yourself or you never grow up. I still have strong feelings for Colum, too. You might as well know that. I have to see him from time to time and we both know, we both have to secretly acknowledge, that we're *parents*, there's an entity somewhere in the hills of Argyll that's half-me, half-him.''

He still said nothing and she said on a note of total resignation, "Well, there it is. It's out now and we have to live with it, one way or another. For what it's worth, I'm sorry, sorry.''

"I—" he said. "I—"

"Christie-Ann doesn't know. That my son is alive. She thinks he died at birth. Please. There's only one thing I ask of you. Don't tell her. Ever.''

"Your mother knows, of course?''

"My mother was the architect of the whole sorry mess. I was only seventeen at the time, Edward, and very, very frightened.''

She, who had never been the first to volunteer touch, touched his hand now. "I know it's been a shock," she acknowledged, "but I had to do something to make you see me as I really am. I want to make the effort for Jasmine's sake. So what do you say? Say something!"

"Was this why you resisted our having a family for so long?"

"I don't know. Well, yes, I suppose there were what Kelsey calls unconscious forces at work."

"I don't really know anything about you," he said wonderingly.

"Yes, you do. You know me perfectly well. Except for that one episode. I'm neither proud nor ashamed of it. I just want it to be accepted. Put on the record. No more lies. I think it's the only way I can have any peace."

"Do you think there's any future for us?" He laid a stress on the last word. She thought his voice had lost tone and timbre, that it was injected with a curious kind of bitter detachment. It was to be the way he spoke to her from then on.

"How should I know? All I know is that wishing gets nothing undone."

"Isobel." Catherine stood at the foot of the stairs and called up. There were sounds of Jasmine throwing some kind of tantrum and above that, Isobel's voice calm and determined and to Catherine, somehow infuriating. As the girl came to the stair-head, Catherine demanded "What's all the row about?"

"Wearing her woolly hat."

"If she doesn't want to wear it, don't insist."

"But she had earache—"

"That was a week ago. Don't molly-coddle. It's nice and warm today."

Isobel said nothing, but it was obvious by the silence as she went back into the nursery that she had given up the tussle. She came downstairs with her still red-faced protagonist, now a sturdy two-and-a-half year old. Catherine kissed her daughter and said, "Mummy see you bedtime, darling. Be good."

"I be good." It was somewhere between indignant assertion and promise. As she walked towards the college, Catherine wondered not for the first time recently whether Isobel was right for the job. She had been a quiet, unassuming girl when she first came. But her voice seemed to have got louder over recent months, her manner more sullen and recalcitrant. Maybe she was tiring of the post.

Catherine would not be altogether sorry if she upped and went. She wasn't irreplaceable.

Isobel strapped Jasmine in to her pushchair and, leaving her just outside the front door where she could watch school-going children through the gate, popped into the downstairs cloakroom and carefully applied lipstick and a little mascara. She ran a comb through her neat, straight, shoulder-length hair and practised a mysterious, pondering smile on her mirror image. She was half-listening all the while for Mr. Elkins' footsteps coming from the morning-room into the hall, where he would pick up his coat, umbrella and brief-case. When he did so, she was there, dithering on the doorstep.

Edward stopped to kiss his daughter. "Where are you two ladies off to?" he demanded, with jocular formality.

"Shops," said Jasmine, briefly. "Get chocolate," she added, hopefully.

Edward smiled at Isobel. He felt it was amazing how the girl had changed from raw, awkward and near-plain into this rather graceful and under-stated person with the compelling smile and gaze that was somehow tender and understanding. A rare thing. He liked her small, supple waist and the competent hands settling in the pushchair handle.

They stood in the sunshine before he got into the car.

"The roses have been lovely," said Isobel Lockhart. "What a shame they're nearly over."

He sniffed a fading bloom. "Do you like flowers, Isobel?"

"Oh, I do."

"And what else? A girl who likes flowers would also like—let me see—poetry, perhaps. I see you liking poetry."

"I don't know much," she confessed. Her swan-like neck turned away and the straight hair fell over her face. He fought a wish to push it back with his free hand.

"Would you like me to lend you a book or two?"

That shy, hasty smile. "Oh yes, Mr. Elkins."

"I'll see what I can find on my shelves." He was suddenly a shade discomfited. He really didn't have all morning to spend standing there in the sunshine, but it had been a very pleasant prelude to the day's hassle.

Isobel stood by while he got into the car and then carefully closed the door for him. "Wave," she said to Jasmine. "Wave to Daddy, like a good girl."

"I've done the windows," said Lizzie Bathgate, "and I've tidied out the pantry. That just leaves me with the kitchen walls to wash down."

Catherine shook her head helplessly. "It's no good saying to you none of it needs doing. You did all that last week." Her mother used work as others used prayers.

"I have my standards."

"What about this letter you've had from Inveraray?" Catherine sat down, her calm composure revealing little of the turmoil she was feeling.

"It's from Catriona."

"And how is Struan?" She kept her voice tonelessly formal.

"He wants to see you."

She got up and walked into the little scullery, picking up a dishcloth and automatically drying the cup and saucer her

170

mother had left draining. Lizzie followed her in, her bright dark eyes crinkled in an effort to read Catherine's reaction.

"I thought it was forever. I thought he was Catriona's for good."

"It's no' Catriona's doing. It's the boy's. He's no' seeing eye-to-eye with his parents about what he's going to do."

"I knew this would happen some day. I've been waiting for it to happen. What do they want him to do?"

"Study for the doctoring or the law."

"And what does he want to do?"

"All he knows he doesn't want to go to university. He thinks he would like to become an actor."

"An actor!"

"Aye, an actor, of a' things. His head's full o' some nonsense about it's being his vocation. If it had been the ministry, I might have seen the sense o' it. But an actor."

"What am I supposed to do? Support him?"

"He thinks you might. Catriona's heart-broken. She feels she's lost him."

"Well, I don't propose to take him away from her. Not after all these years. What would I say to him? He's like a total stranger."

"I'll write to her," said Lizzie, relievedly.

"No." She clenched one hand inside the other. "No. I'll see him. I'll talk to him. Tell her I'll meet him in Glasgow."

"Do you want me to come with you?"

"Would you like to?"

"I still remember the way he looked up at me, the day he was born. As if to say 'What have you got me into'?"

Catherine looked at her mother. It was the first intimation she had had that her mother had felt anything on the fateful day.

In the bus going into Glasgow on the day Catherine was to meet her son, both women sat with fixed, strained expressions. Lizzie had become stout, barrel-y in late middle-age. She dressed with the formal care of the older generation, her fawn blouse toning in with her brown suit and the whole with her brown felt hat with its small, turned-up brim and grosgrain bow. Her shoes had been carefully polished. Catherine wore a pale blue two-piece with a double strand of pearls but like most younger women of the time she back-combed her hair and had given up wearing a hat.

Lizzie said, as if this was a conversation that had gone on for a long time (as indeed it had, in both women's subconscious) "If I had let you keep him, you'd never have had a house in Hawktoun Road."

"As if it would have mattered," Catherine responded.

"Nor a decent man."

"Colum would have been a decent man."

"As he's been to our Christie-Ann," said Lizzie, with the utmost disdainful scorn.

"I never asked you to come with me," Catherine burst out. As so often now when she was with her mother, her emotions could scarcely be contained. The anger and resentment seemed to surge out of her. Her hands tingled and the acid rose in her gullet from the effort of containing herself. Lizzie knew it and the colour rose in her own face as she defended herself.

"Don't think I haven't seen what happens. A lassie gets landed, she puts a face on things but no matter how well she

173

manages, she's never allowed to forget what she'd done. Aye, and the finger gets pointed at the innocent bairn too."

"You forget I had the option. I could have married Colum when I was old enough. Even when he came out the army."

"And lived on what? The wind?"

"The sum total is you hate the Brodies."

"I was right there." Lizzie's jaw looked as though it had been set in concrete. "All the flim-flam, the fluttering of hearts, the Hollywood stuff, how long do you think it lasts? What lasts is meat on the table, clothes on your back."

"You don't know what love is."

"I never had it. I had a selfish man who let me rise out of childbed to go and scrub stairs. Who went out with the whippet when I cried with the pain of ulcers on my legs and turned his back to the wall when you or Christie-Ann had the fever or the croup."

"Colum's not like that."

"Ask Christie-Ann. She'll tell you."

They had arranged to meet Struan at the Corn Exchange, opposite the Central Station, but as they approached the

174

restaurant Catherine's stride slowed and eventually she grasped her mother's arm and said, "I can't do it."

"What do you mean?" Lizzie's face was as grim as her own.

"I can't face it."

"He'll be sitting there," said Lizzie, "the laddie, waiting for us."

Catherine felt inside her handbag and brought out a large sealed envelope. She handed it to her mother.

"What's this?"

"Money. Quite a bit. To pay for him going to London."

"Give it to him yourself."

"Mother, go in and see him. Tell him —tell him I wish him all the best, but that I'm not well, I'm sick, tell him something."

"A fine time to change your tune." Lizzie stood irresolute, studying her daughter's face.

Catherine said, "Just to see him, then let him go again, that's what I can't face."

Lizzie dithered for a moment or two then stuffed the envelope into her capacious black handbag. Unconsciously, she squared her shoulders.

"Where will you go?"

"I'll go some place for a coffee and see you at the bus station in an hour."

"You're being stupid." Lizzie looked at her daughter and saw she was as pale as death. "Very well," she conceded, "I'll do what you ask."

Catherine watched her mother enter the restaurant and then instead of retracing her own steps walked with a kind of fearful, timid fascination to see if she could scan the interior. She saw Lizzie merge into the middle distance between tables and then a dark boy with hair standing up in a kind of quiff rise from a table.

It was at that point she turned and walked away as fast as her legs would carry her.

Christie-Ann manoeuvred the pushchair with Lindsay in it into the lobby at the *Courier*. Well wrapped up against the wind and rain in scarves and covers, Lindsay had fallen fast asleep, her face damp and apple-red. She was getting too old to be pushed about, but it was a long walk to the *Courier* office and it was getting late.

Leaving the child in the lobby, Christie-Ann pushed open the office door and in the unsatisfactory light saw her husband working at his desk. "Still there?" she said. Almost without looking up he finished a piece of subbing, then threw down his pencil and sat back.

"What brings *you* here?" he demanded on a truculent note.

"What do you think? The shops are closing and I'm waiting for money to buy the weekend food."

"You mean, you thought if you got here in time you could stop me going to the dogs. Too late, lovie. I'm going."

Christie-Ann kept her voice low. "No," she protested, "you're not going tonight, Colum. I'm not having any arguments about what a win could do for us. I'm sick of arguments."

"Well, you know what you can do."

"And I'm sick of your innuendoes. One day, I'm warning you, I'll take you up on them. I'll leave and take the children with me."

"Go and stay with your mother, will you?"

"I'll find somewhere. Not with my

mother. And I'm going no more cap in hand to Catherine, either. You can take her hand-outs if you like but I don't want anybody's charity. I'm going to be more like Catherine. I'll find a job, be independent."

"You make no allowances for my disabilities," he said. "If I could afford the car repairs I'd get around that much quicker—"

"Catherine gave you money for the car. You gambled it." She looked at him in open contempt. "She paid for you to have your novel typed, too."

"There it is." He pointed to a fat package lying on an in-tray. "It needs more work done on it, they say."

"That's what the last one said, too."

"There you are, then."

"What am I to do?"

He took money from his pockets, counted out two notes and some silver and handed it to her.

"It isn't enough. I owe the butcher."

"It'll have to do."

"So your disabilities will still permit you to go to the dogs?"

178

"I have to trust in a turn of luck. It's got to come some time."

"Come home. Learn sense."

"Not tonight." He did not look at her.

She pushed Lindsay back out into the wind and the rain and the child still did not wake. Her mind whirled with the need to stretch the pittance he had given her to the best possible advantage. She was free to weep tears of frustration because they mingled with the rain. But she felt something else, too. A hardening, a resolution. This kind of existence could not go on.

7

LINDSAY COLLINS *née* Brodie stopped her smart little Standard car in Dounhead Main Street and got out. She had a vague recollection of being pushed along here in a pram on a wet and windy night to her father's office, when she must have been about four or five. Twenty years ago. Just before her mother had taken her and Clare south on the train to London. God, they'd lived in some crummy dumps, on social security, till her mother trained as a fashion buyer and got the well-paid, secure job she was still doing.

She couldn't bear to look at where the *Courier* had been. When the paper had gone to the wall someone had bought the premises and turned them into a bakery.

Aunt Catherine's college was a different matter. Ah, there it was, much extended since its early days. Nowadays it not only gave girls a sound commercial training but taught computer skills and language courses. You had to admire Aunt Catherine. Even if you did not have to like her.

Lindsay got back in the car and drove towards her grandmother's house, where she had arranged to meet the others. Object: sharing out the few pieces of china and jewellery. Yesterday's funeral was still fresh in her mind. She had been surprised to find what a strong emotional grip the old lady, her grandmother had had on most of them. Personally she could only remember being told to keep sticky hands off the furniture, to wipe her feet and not to drop crumbs. Yet there must have been more to the old girl than autocracy and bad temper. Her two daughters had circled round her mementoes after the funeral with bird-like cries of sorrow and bereavement that were genuinely heart-rending. Yet they had both feared and at times hated their mother, as hard and sour, Lindsay reflected, as an under-ripe gooseberry. But yesterday it had been Aunt Catherine saying, "Perhaps as the elder *I* should have her wedding ring" and Mum looking mutinous, even murderous, as she'd staked her claim for the engagement ring. Lindsay had got an authentic whiff of the sheer engine power of sibling rivalry. Not that she and Clare weren't the same when they were together.

She'd been glad to have her cousin Jasmine to talk to. Clare had not come up for the funeral, not being able to get time off from her newspaper job, and Lindsay's husband, Jack, an oilman, was working in the Middle East.

"I don't remember what she was about," she'd confessed to Jasmine, with a nod towards the coffin.

"She was a bit of an old Tartar," said Jasmine, "but I'll miss her."

"Miss her?"

"Well, you know, Mum and Dad are always busy with their careers and she was always there to talk to. She'd go on about the old days, Grandpa in the war, that sort of thing."

And then Jasmine, later, after the ham tea, had said something quite strange; "Last week when the drugs were making her mind wander a bit, she made me get a snapshot out of the drawer in the chiffonier there. It was in an envelope all by itself and it just said 'Struan'. I said

'Who's that?' and she said after a bit, 'You'll have to ask your mother'."

"Did you ask Aunt Catherine about it?"

Jasmine had assumed an evasive, half-guilty expression.

"I couldn't. You know Mum."

"No, I don't very well."

"You can't just talk to her."

"Why not?"

"It—it's what we're like. Not very confiding."

Lindsay had looked at her cousin a little more closely and decided she was in need of befriending. She was a stringy, pale girl with a habit of shuffling her stance uncertainly. Today if Jasmine didn't do it she'd bring up the business of the photograph and get them talking about it. It was really quite intriguing and she could see Jasmine had been having a good old brood about it.

The little cottage where Lizzie Bathgate had lived out her life seemed small and half-derelict, although no doubt it would sell swiftly enough and be trendied up before you could say knife.

Catherine, Christie-Ann and Jasmine

were already there. Christie-Ann, in a smart knitted two-piece of a soft purply colour, looked up as her daughter entered and said, "Look, Lindsay, your grandmother had this old teapot from *her* grandmother. Would you like it?"

"What about Jasmine? Or Aunt Catherine?"

"They've already picked some cups and saucers. It's our side's turn now."

"Surely we don't regard ourselves as 'sides'," Lindsay demurred, with what came out as a nervous laugh. But she knew what her mother meant. All through the visit there had been this sense of restraint, of watching points. She looked at Catherine in her chic black suit, her hair immaculately set and felt a frisson of antipathy. Catherine was so *controlled*, so visibly a person of some importance, used to giving orders, to being obeyed. Yesterday at the funeral there had been no sense of shared grief between her and Uncle Edward Elkins. He'd been coolly formal, she'd sent nothing outwards even in her grief. Poor Jasmine, Lindsay thought. But I'm going to help her solve the enigma of the photograph. What have I got to lose?

"Do you remember, Catherine," Christie-Ann was saying now, "how Mother used to make us stand on this little stool to wash ourselves in the scullery?" She said to Jasmine and Lindsay, "We had no piped hot water then."

"I always got the neck of my vest wet," said Catherine reflectively, "and then it would chafe afterwards. So would the back of my knees where I hadn't dried properly."

"The towels were old flour sacking," said Christie-Ann. "No wonder they wouldn't dry."

Jasmine and Lindsay looked at each other sympathetically and Lindsay said robustly, "We mustn't let this memory lane business get out of hand. Aunt Catherine," she continued on a determined note, "did you see the photograph Grandma showed Jasmine? Of a boy called Struan?"

Catherine's head rose slowly from the war medals of her father that she had been examining. There was a faint tone of red on her neck.

"What photograph?"

"It was here," said Jasmine, quickly. "In the drawer of the chiffonier." She pulled the drawer open but it was empty.

"You cleared the drawer this morning, Catherine, didn't you?" said Christie-Ann.

"I may have done. Oh, yes. But there was no photograph that I can remember."

"There was yesterday," said Jasmine positively. "I looked. And Grandma made me get it out last week and said 'Ask your mother about it.' She passed a hand over it and then she kissed it and asked me to put it back."

"Maybe it was a nephew or something," said Catherine. "Mother's brothers nearly all emigrated and she had a job remembering who was where."

"It didn't look an old photograph," said Jasmine. "It was of a boy of about seventeen, with a kind of quiff of dark hair." She rummaged about in the empty drawer, even taking it out and looking behind it, her air of mystification growing.

"I never saw it," said Catherine positively. "But maybe it'll turn up. I would quite like to see it. Solve the mystery." And she laughed.

"I don't know why I should bother asking," said Christie-Ann, "after all this time. But what is going to happen about Colum?"

The two girls had gone off for a walk together and Catherine and Christie-Ann were sitting on either side of the fire in their mother's cottage, while the shadows gathered and thickened outside. Large grocery boxes filled with china, books and bric-à-brac and clothes testified to an afternoon's steady work.

"He's pretty frail, after the last operation on his hip," said Catherine. She gazed towards her sister, scarcely able to make out her face. Yet neither made a move to put on the light or draw the curtains.

"I still feel responsibility for him, despite the separation and everything," said Christie-Ann. "I mean, money broke us up, or rather the lack of it. Nothing else. He was a hopeless provider."

"Lucille was talking of bringing him home from the hospital to stay with her."

"I was thinking, Catherine, he could have this cottage—"

"Mother would whirl in her grave."

"Yes, but it's ours now, to decide what to do with. Lucille could look in on him, he could possibly have a home help."

"I'm not against the idea."

"The girls go on at me about him. You'd think it was *us* who'd let *him* down. It would really please them to think their father had a place of his own. They'd be able to come up and stay with him."

"What about you?"

"Oh, no. I don't think so."

"You wouldn't come back?"

"I couldn't. I don't talk the language any more. Besides, after a while they take away your passport."

"I sense something more. Maybe a someone . . ."

"Yes. I live with a someone."

"Do the girls approve?"

"I don't think they approve or disapprove. They just accept. Times they are a-changing, Catherine."

"Oh, yes. I know that. The permissive society reached us here, too." There was a slightly acid tone to her voice. "Well, we'll agree about Colum and the cottage. That's if he wants it. Will you go and see him, or will I?"

"Maybe it would be best if we went together."

"Do you think we could find somewhere to have a cup of tea?" demanded Lindsay. Her cousin had walked her off her feet and was pooh-poohing any idea of catching a bus back home. The boring monotony of Lowland suburbia was depressing her.

"There's an Italian café," said Jasmine. They ordered ice-creams instead of tea, followed by frothy coffee. "I'll be putting on weight," Lindsay groaned.

Jasmine said, "I never need to worry about that." Both girls secretly peered in the cafe's mirrors. Both had long, almost waist-length hair in the seventies manner, Jasmine's a satiny mouse colour and Lindsay's fine and molten gold, as her Aunt Catherine's had once been. Each wore heavy eye make-up, mascara and shadow, but were pale-lipped. Their tights were pale-coloured too, and their Shetland jumpers had a fashionably shrunken look.

"I think I'll ask Dad about the photograph," said Jasmine. She had a tendency to harp, Lindsay thought, to worry away at a topic that verged on the neurotic. She had almost forgotten the photograph herself.

"Do you get on with your Dad," she asked curiously, "better than you do your mother?"

"I hardly see either of them. He's forever abroad on computer business and she eats, sleeps and lives the college. But yes, he and I are a bit alike. I think they're disappointed I wasn't more academic. Two tycoons for parents and I end up in the tax office. But it suits me. I don't want challenges."

"I'd have thought you might want your own place."

"I might have done, but I keep a kind of balance in the family. If I left, Mum and Dad's relationship would crumble."

"You think so?" Lindsay looked at her cousin in shocked surprise.

"Oh yes. I've been the cement in the family for as long as I can remember. He had an affair with my nanny, you know. Isobel Lockhart. I think he still meets her in Glasgow sometimes and to my certain knowledge they've had holidays together. About ten years ago Mum found out and it looked like curtains—you know, divorce and all that. But I started doing badly at school, truanting even, and they decided to stay together for the sake of the child. Little old moi."

"That's all very well." Lindsay stirred her coffee with some concentration. "But it's a bit sick to draw you into their tangled web. Suppose you want to marry?"

"The man *I* love is married."

"Jasmine? Do *they* know?"

"Of course not. I'm schooled in keeping secrets."

Lindsay said, "Jasmine!" again, even more reproachfully.

"I always seem to pick the unsuitable."

"Will he divorce?"

"I don't know. Anyhow, as I was saying about the parents . . . they're very conventional. They care deeply about what people say, Mum especially. And he can't really let go. He's waiting for the Snow Maiden to melt—that's Mum—and she won't. She never will. These days her health is bad— she gets a lot of migraine. She can't help herself."

"You have a lot of insight."

"Enough to know people can get into the most frightful emotional morass. You know my mother and your father had an affair when they were young? Oh, yes, when the battle between Isobel and Mum was at the ding-dong stage, I found out about it. Seems it had been the talk of the steamy, as they say, in the old days. Isobel delighted in telling me. Your dad came back from the war and found Mum had married somebody else. Namely Ed. Elkins, Esquire."

"I think I'd had an inkling from mum about that. When we went south. She let slip once that she wished she'd never married Dad, because she'd always been second-best. She hasn't been to see him yet. I have. She doesn't write to him. I do. So does Clare."

They looked at each other soberly.

"Are you happy with Jack?" asked Jasmine.

"The sex is good."

"Thank goodness for that. I wouldn't like to think we were all screwed up, every last one of us." They sipped in reflective silence.

"I *am* going to ask Dad about that photograph," said Jasmine. "I've got an almost paranormal feeling about it."

"I think you're being a bit fanciful about it. Who could it be of?"

"The thing is," said Jasmine, "it disappeared. It was there and then it wasn't."

"It probably got thrown out with old papers and stuff that didn't matter."

"We'll see."

As Catherine drove towards Hillmyres Hospital where she had arranged to meet her sister she thought of the time Christie-Ann had taken the children and left Colum.

Christie-Ann had said nothing to any of them. She had simply made her plans. One day she was there and the next not. Colum had come to the house in Hawktoun Road to see if Catherine could shed any light on the matter. In its increasingly well-heeled ambience he had looked like a broken-down busker.

At first there hadn't been an address. Christie-Ann had eventually let them know she was all right, but not where she was living. Guilt about the children had made

Colum do something he had never done before. Drink before noon. And then heavily before bedtime.

She stopped the car because her legs were trembling so much she was afraid it would affect her driving. *Struan!* She had not allowed herself to think about him for so long, but at that time it had been different. And she could talk to no-one, no-one. She drew deep, shuddering breaths now, from the abdomen, forcing herself to relax. If there was a prospect of getting Colum out of the hospital, she had to keep herself from getting nervous and over-emotional. *Deep breaths. Deep breaths. You are warm and relaxed. Your arms and legs are heavy and warm.* In a little she felt enough in charge of herself to start the car once again.

The memories kept coming back, though if she kept away from Struan she could edit them in her head. She had gone over them often enough, in all conscience. At the *Courier* things had gone from bad to worse. She could not keep bailing Colum out of the debts he had got into and she could not reason with him over his gambling and his drinking. The young reporter Brian had stayed on till the bitter end, for a wage that would have been laughable had it not been pitiable. And then Colum's war injuries began to play him up and a series of operations began. The *Courier* lurched from crisis to crisis.

She had had her own problems compounded when the affair between Isobel and Edward came to a head. The girl having hysterics in the nursery, her father coming to the door and threatening to tear Edward's head off his shoulders. Edward using the situation—she saw now —to try and bring about a *rapprochement* between them after the years of what you could only call half-marriage. And poor Jasmine, reacting like litmus paper to everything that went on around her.

Somehow she had wound up the *Courier*, salvaged a little money for Colum and reached an accommodation with Edward. Isobel was sacked, of course, and Catherine found a housekeeper, Mrs. Bendle, less censorious or nosey than the average Dounhead citizen because she was taken up with her own interests of spiritualism and palmistry. Out of guilt, she supposed, Catherine made sure Edward lived in a comfortable and well-run household, where meals arrived on time, his clothes were looked after and his child could bring her friends. Habit wrought its own transformation. They functioned somehow as a family and Jasmine gave up some of her nervous behaviour and learned to take what she could from each parent. But Catherine's salvation had been the college. She had clung to her business and her growing status in the community. Despite everything. Because there was a cool, hard, calculating part of her that needed to know she would survive without help from anyone. That required to give orders not take them. That wanted efficiency, success, that were self-obvious. "You're waiting for praise from Mother," Christie-Ann had once said when they were being analytical. Not that it ever came. Even in her present mourning, she had not yet reached the point of forgiveness where her mother was concerned. Hate and grief could co-exist.

She had not been able to bring herself to see Colum very often these last years. Her own marriage worked in proportion to the amount of time she thought about

Colum. She still felt compassion and love wrung from her endlessly as regards him. She still wanted to go to him, put her arms around him and make him over again. She knew how irrational this was, but she was accustomed to the irrationality of her emotions as far as he was concerned. To her, the essential Colum had not changed at all. He still had more goodness, more generosity, more grace under pressure than anyone she had ever known. And he still loved her first and unconditionally. No mention was ever made of this, but they both knew it. She only had to look at his face to know it. When she looked at him, everything that was important emotionally was an open book, there to be read, though only by her. He had simply been handed a life-card of such complexity he could not have been expected to play it to advantage. But apart from alluding to the growing-up of his daughters away from him, he never allowed bitterness to creep into anything he said. When they talked about Christie-Ann, he wore a grave and guilty look. "I ran away from her," was all he would say, "before she left me. I ran away from her in my mind."

How difficult life is, thought Catherine, as she got out of the car in the hospital car park. The life we live on the surface and the life we live underneath. The life we want and the life we get. The conviction that it was the same for most people, maybe for everyone, made her feel more tender-hearted to the world at large. And perhaps a little brave.

"Oh, God," said Christie-Ann, tugging at Catherine's arm. "Is that him? I can't go in."

"Come on," said Catherine firmly, leading the way. Colum sat up in bed, a cage over his legs. Where he had once been fresh-faced and ruddy, he was hospital-pale. He still had the tumbling mop of hair, but it was greying. He gave them a smile Christie-Ann could only think of as twisted and rueful. She had not been prepared for his, and certainly not her own, vulnerability.

Formally she put out her hand. "I'm sorry about your mother," he said.

"Yes," she answered, sitting down, suddenly a voyager without a compass.

"You're looking well, Christie-Ann."

"You've seen Lindsay."

"A smasher," he said, gently.

Catherine was pouring some lemon barley water into a tumbler. She held it out to him wordlessly, claiming the intimacy of the one who had not gone away. "I see you need some paper hankies," she stated. "I'll get you some."

"You've had a hard time, Colum. What's the latest bulletin?"

"They're going to get me some of those elbow crutches."

"For permanent use?"

"Well—next year there could be another operation. Or two."

"And then?"

"I've learned not to prognosticate. We'll have to wait and see. I would just like to be, shall we say, half-independent. I think the book that's been brewing all these years is going to get written at last. Maybe by the time Clare gets married, I'll be able to give her a portion towards the mortgage. Lindsay, too, though from the sound of it she's got a husband who's a good provider."

"More important, Lindsay can provide for herself."

"Yes. Oh yes."

Catherine pulled up a chair on the opposite side of the bed to her sister.

"Colum, we've been talking, Christie-Ann and I, and we've decided you should have Mother's cottage to live in. It's near Lucille and it's not too far from me—we can look in to see how you are."

He looked from one to the other.

"You're serious," he said at last.

"Just till you write that best-seller and can afford something better." Christie-Ann could not look at the glimmering tenderness on her sister's face. She had wanted to tell Colum their decision herself.

"That's all right, Mrs. Bendle. We'll go ahead and eat." Edward Elkins poked his head round the kitchen door and addressed his housekeeper. "Mrs. Elkins won't be back till later."

He faced his daughter across the dining-room table as Mrs. Bendle served the soup. Scotch broth. He stirred the barley reflectively with his spoon, watching it spin satisfactorily in the small, man-made vortex. Good word, that. *Vortex.*

"Eat up, Daddy," Jasmine admonished him, as though he were a small boy. She checked that Mrs. Bendle had closed the door behind her and said in a carefully-lowered tone that was almost conspiratorial, "There's something I want to ask you about."

"Ask." That last of the barley was gone. He gave her his attention.

"When Grannie was fuddled with drugs, last week, just before she died, she made me get a photograph out of the chiffonier drawer."

She had fine hands, his daughter, he thought irrelevantly. She was so like him with her slight, straight-backed physique, her direct, questioning look, he never had to search for a key to her moods as he did with her mother, even now. He waited.

"It was of a boy, well, a teenager, and the name on the envelope was Struan. Grannie said, 'Ask your mother to tell you about him,' but Mummie disclaims any knowledge of him. I'm intrigued. I wondered if you knew a Struan in the family." She was playing with her knife, balancing it on her forefinger. Mrs. Bendle came in and took out the soup-plates, then

201

placed a parsley-graced plate of fried and bread-crumbed fish before the diners and carried in creamed potatoes and vegetables to accompany it. She liked to do this with a flourish, knowing her cooking was to their liking, that she had not forgotten any little preferences such as a grating of nutmeg over the potatoes. Once again she withdrew, almost balletic in her sense of usefulness.

"Daddy?" The litmus paper that was Jasmine's mind changed colour, darkened. Outwardly her father's expression hadn't changed, but the hands on the eating implements had gone flaccid, as though they would be useless in such everyday pursuits as cutting up and conveying morsels to the mouth.

"I don't know the name," said Edward. "It's a name that means nothing to me."

"Why would Grannie say what she did?"

"What was your mother's explanation?"

"That Grannie was confused. That he might have been a great-nephew, descended from one of Grannie's brothers who emigrated. I don't think so, though. I smell a family secret."

"What kind of secret?"

"How would I know? Oh, I'm not making a big song scena out of it," Jasmine disclaimed. "I'd just like to know."

"Where is the photograph now?"

"That's another mystery. It just disappeared. Eat up your fish, Daddy. Remember the starving millions."

"I didn't think he would be like that." Christie-Ann blew her nose into a tiny inadequate hankie, while Catherine watched her almost stonily. When she had stopped weeping, Catherine at length started the car.

"You haven't seen him for so long," she reminded her sister.

"You might have told me, Catherine."

"I did tell you. About the operations."

"Not about the—winnowing. There's not much more than spirit left, is there? He's all eyes. Just eyes. Can bloody moving shrapnel do that to a man? It's as though a gust of wind could blow him away." The tears flooded forth again. "I want him out of there, Catherine. He must take the cottage."

"You heard what Sister said. He would need a lot of support. Nurses would come in."

"I could give up the flat in London, I could come back. I owe it to the girls. It's what they would want."

"Don't be silly," said Catherine sharply. She was manoeuvring out of the hospital car park and endeavouring not to clip the wing of a badly positioned Rover, but as they spun along the wide new highway back to Dounhead she elaborated. "You can't say you have a marriage after twenty years."

"It wouldn't be a marriage in the way you're thinking," Christie-Ann argued. "It would be patient and nurse. I *could* look after him. And if he's serious about the book, I could type it out for him—"

"Surely I'm the typist in the family," Catherine burst out. "I think he would look to me to do it for him."

"What about Edward's feelings?"

"What feelings? Look, how would you live?"

"On his pension."

"After what you've been used to, as a

204

working woman? Holidays in Gran Canaria and Miami. Nice clothes. Hairdoes."

Christie-Ann sniffed, then said more soberly, "I would have thought you'd want him looked after." The inference hung heavily in the air. "You, who have never uttered a critical word against him."

"What about the someone you live with?"

"He'll be gone, one of these days. He happens to be quite a bit younger. It wouldn't be right for us to get hitched."

"Has he asked you?"

"As a matter of fact, yes."

"Well, then?"

"He's fifteen years younger."

"That's quite a compliment."

"It's a hellish moral dilemma. I know it wouldn't be right, but I'm tempted."

"I see."

"You're not going back on what we agreed about the cottage, are you?"

"Of course not."

"Then I might very well stay for a while. I'm not saying for good. But for a while."

Catherine decided to keep quiet. Christie-Ann was over-reacting because of the shock of seeing Colum after so long. Twenty years! It was ridiculous of her to think of the marriage as valid after all that time. Yet she'd held his hand in the ward and he had seemed genuinely moved to see her.

Catherine did not know how to cope with her own innermost feelings. When she got home, she would go to bed, take some of her pills, keep away from Edward and Jasmine. She could feel the pounding nausea of migraine take hold. Christie-Ann *couldn't* live with Colum again. It was an offence against nature. He belonged to her, Catherine. She would have organized his life in the cottage for him, so that he had all the help he needed.

She was glad Christie-Ann and Lindsay were staying at the cottage and not with her at Hawktoun Road, although she had invited them to do so. It meant now she could drop Christie-Ann off and have a little time on her own to compose herself. To think.

But Christie-Ann stood at the open car door and pleaded with her.

"Come in, Catherine. I need to talk some more."

They made scrambled egg and ate it from plates off their knees.

By this time, Catherine's flood of emotion had subsided into bewilderment. She looked at Christie-Ann, crisp and cosmopolitan, listened to her rounded vowels and thought: she could never really belong here again. She has changed too much. Surely she realizes it? It wasn't just appearance, it was the way she thought, her attitudes. In some ways, she looked a young girl. If that was what having a younger lover did for you, then it was to be recommended.

Christie-Ann poured each of them some coffee, sat down and crossed her elegant London legs. She said, "Isn't it funny how seldom we've managed to see each other in all those years? You've never been to my latest flat. You don't know what it's like, living in London now. If you go out, you have to take a taxi home. People get mugged all the time. Our Marxist council is run by thugs and bully-boys. I don't know if I want to stay on there in any case."

"*He's mine*," was all Catherine could think, with an aberrant wildness. "You can't come back to Colum because he doesn't belong to you." And she might have been seventeen, and straight from being with Colum for the first time, for all her self, her real self, listened to the acquired wisdom of the years between.

8

"DAD," said Jasmine. "Don't go straight off to your study, please. Couldn't we talk?"

They had finished their coffee in the lounge and she had sent Mrs. Bendle away, saying they didn't want the curtains drawn yet.

"Your mother's bound to be in soon. Isn't there something on the box?"

"I said, I want to talk." Jasmine was adamant. "You know something about this Struan whose snapshot I saw. And I want the information."

"I'm not sure I can give you it."

"Why?"

"Because it appertains to your mother's life. Not mine."

There was a shocked silence. Then Jasmine said to the shadowy space between them, "Are you telling me . . . ? I mean, I've juggled with all kinds of conjectures and the only one that holds water . . . I mean, women have babies, sometimes, before marriage. Was that what happened, Dad?"

"Yes."

"And was it Colum Brodie's?"

"Yes."

"And where is he now? My—my half-brother?"

"I can't give you the answer to that because I don't know it. Struan was adopted by second cousins of your mother's who lived somewhere in Argyll. The break was supposed to be final. That's all I know."

"By God," said Jasmine furiously, "this family knows how to keep a secret—"

"Your mother was trying to protect us and her sister. She had been trained in secrecy by your grandmother. You know the fearful clacking tongues round here."

"But when she had the baby, it must have been noticed."

"No. She was sent away to the cousins and came back when it was all over. Colum was told at first the baby had been born dead."

"That was wicked."

"Your mother was seventeen. Your grandmother dominated her totally. Your mother's whole life has been a struggle to break free from that domination."

"She doesn't deserve you. You've put up with her nerves, her migraine, her obsession with the college. Why haven't you left her, Daddy? You could have made a better life for yourself with Isobel Lockhart."

"I don't know. I took her for better or worse."

"You love her."

"That must be it."

Jasmine sat down at the small table by the window, her head supported by one hand under her chin. "I've just realized. Struan is half-brother to Lindsay, too— and Clare. What a mess. Did Aunt Kissie—?"

Edward said with the first sign of irritability, "Don't go on, Jasmine. The story told to Christie-Ann was that the baby had died. Your mother wanted to keep it that way."

"So she's lied and lied and lied. Even about the photograph. I'll bet she took that, out of the drawer."

"It was *her* affair, don't you see that? How often have you told us we don't own

211

you? Well, by the same token, your mother's life is her own."

"Are you talking about me, by any chance?"

So intense had their preoccupation been that Edward and Jasmine had not heard Catherine come in. She stood now in the doorway, unloosening a scarf, her camel jacket half-off one shoulder. She stepped haltingly into the room, automatically clicking on one sidelight the better to see them. She was greeted with silence.

She walked back into the hall and hung up her coat. Looked at her hair in the mirror. Made the tidying gestures women have made since time immemorial. Came back in to the room. Closed the door.

"I heard 'your mother's life is her own'." She appealed to Edward. "I presume you meant it? You were supporting me? What's it all about?"

"It's about your son," said Jasmine.

Catherine, whose stance till then had been stoic, if questioning, appeared to break up before their eyes. She wrung her hands. She looked wildly from one to the other. She sat down on one chair and got up and moved to another. Jasmine gazed at her mercilessly.

"Mother, you may have thought you had the right to keep this to yourself. But did it ever occur to you I had rights as well? I grew up lonely—so lonely you'll never know—and I used to dream about a brother or sister. Well, I want to know now. I want to know about Struan, how old he is, what he does. There's a bit of me in him. A bit of him in me. That makes me less of a loner for a start!" Jasmine was weeping and wringing her hands now, as though in unison.

Into the maelstrom the telephone rang like a bell for seconds out. Jasmine picked it up and said "Yes?" in abrupt discouragement.

"Lindsay? Why don't you and your mother come over here? Yes, if you want to talk about Colum. I've got something to tell you about him. And the photograph. Prepare yourself for shocks." She put the receiver down and laughed, a grating, ugly sound. "I've let the cat among the pigeons now, all right."

Christie-Ann stood irresolutely outside her

husband's ward. Her hair, which had been so smartly styled when she left London, was limp and unkempt. She hadn't even bothered to fasten her coat or put on lipstick. She had been impelled to try and see Colum immediately she had learned about his son. Almost as though she wanted a disclaimer. But, of course, there wasn't going to be a disclaimer. After Jasmine and Lindsay had talked on the phone last night, Edward had told them everything. He had been very matter-of-fact, probably for the girl's sake. He hadn't looked directly at her. Not once. As for Catherine, she had listened, interjected and then, looking crushed and defeated, had taken to her bed.

She had been very, very angry. It had been like taking her own marriage away from her and whatever Catherine thought, about the exclusivity of the relationship between herself and Colum, for a while the marriage had been all she had wanted. Colum with his non-judgemental nature, his openness, his gentleness. If only the paper had paid, if only he had not stayed so long with his dreams or given in to the wilder dreams of saving the situation through gambling.

God knows, she saw him every time she saw his daughters. Clare had inherited his looks and his way with words, Lindsay his giving nature and the sharpness of his perception. Well, they were both independent now, the girls, and she had thought for a little it would be possible to come back. To live with him, even work to keep them both. Because of the mysterious bonding of family. Because he would be there when she got in at night. The one she lived with would go away; she had always known he would. He was too young, she should never have taken up with him in the first place. Lately her girlhood inhibitions had come back to haunt her. Possibly she had seen her return as a kind of penance for the stupidities she had committed over the years. Liberation was no use to those already ensnared by their upbringing.

What could she say to him? *You can't have the cottage, I'm taking back everything I offered.* Yes, that. But more. She wanted to wound and hurt in the way that she had been wounded and hurt.

A nurse came through the swing doors, looked suspiciously at her and inquired if she could help. She thanked her, said no, she was all right, and walked in and up to Colum's bed with its contraptions to save his legs and beside it the cabinet with its lime juice and water jug and paperbacks.

He had been far away, in some distant place of contemplation, despite the newspaper in front of him open at the crossword. He went red, like a boy, straightened his bedclothes and smiled at her.

"Christie-Ann! I didn't expect you." He looked at her set face and inquired immediately, "Is there something the matter? What's wrong?"

She composed herself on the chair beside him before she spoke, smoothing her gloves and silk scarf.

"What is it?" he asked again.

"We had a bit of blood-letting last night. At Catherine and Edward's. And it came out about the boy. About Struan. And you and Catherine keeping it from me, all these years, that he was alive."

He made a tentative effort to take her

hand, could not quite reach it and gave up.

"It was to save you pain," he said abruptly.

"When did you know about him? Exactly." She pinned him with her gaze, demanding no evasions.

"I knew about the child being alive, and not stillborn as I'd been told, when I was going to marry you. Catherine thought I should know."

"She told you because she wanted to stop us marrying, right? She couldn't have you herself but nobody else was supposed to have a look-in."

"It's all water under the bridge, Kissie," he said sadly. "And happened a long time ago."

"She still acts as though she owns you, though. I don't know how she does it. Edward's on a string, nothing but a puppet. You should have seen him last night. The girls were all for having a go at Catherine. He would have none of it. 'I think you should rest, my love. You have the college in the morning.' And that beaten look she takes on sometimes. Filling her hot water bottle and saying 'My

217

head can take no more.' She puts out that she's a frail flower. Frail! Not her."

"Emotionally, she is. Very frail. From the minute they took Struan away from her, she started paying the price. Don't let your natural anger blind you to what your sister has suffered."

"She has suffered! What about me?"

"You're tougher, Christie-Ann. You didn't have your spirit broken, but that's what happened to Catherine."

"How do you know," she demanded, "what happened to me? What happened to me was that I always—always had to play second fiddle."

"Maybe you were too close, you two."

"I sometimes think sisterhood is the hardest relationship. It's where everything hurts. I can get over other jealousies, but never what I feel for Catherine."

"*Try.*"

"Look what she's done to Edward. I could hate her for that alone."

"Edward had options."

"She's got money, ability, position. What more does she want?"

He did not answer. He waited while the strong tide of her feelings rose in her and washed over into tears. At last she put away her handkerchief and powdered her nose, "I came to tell you—I thought for a bit that I'd come back and live in Mother's cottage with you. Take you out of here. It would have eased the girls' minds about you. And I don't care for—for London any more."

"I wouldn't have let you do that."

She might not have heard what he said, for all the effect it registered. "But after this—no, I couldn't do it. This was betrayal and even the girls see that. Get your lovely Catherine, the one who is so magic, so wonderful, to sort things out for you. I don't want anything more to do with you."

She looked at him and saw he had gone very pale and for a quick, rational moment, she wondered if she had gone too far, upset him needlessly.

"I'll go," she said quickly. "The girls will keep in touch."

"That means when he married me, he knew about his son," said Christie-Ann. "That is what I can't get over. That he didn't tell me, then or ever."

219

"I tried to stop you. Nothing would. Not then." Catherine's voice was spent and low. "You were determined to show that anything I can do, you can do better. Even to having my man."

The eddying whirlwind of emotions stirred up by last night's revelations and recriminations was by no means spent. Christie-Ann had come from the hospital. She looked distraught. Earlier, Jasmine had gone off to work pale and hollow-eyed, accompanied by her father. For once, Catherine had not gone to the college.

"It's changed everything," said Christie-Ann. "I can't live with a man capable of such duplicity."

"It wouldn't have worked anyway," said Catherine quietly. "You've got fed-up with London, but coming back here isn't the answer. Living with Colum, especially as he is now, isn't the answer. You've been apart twenty years, Christie-Ann."

"It's poor Edward I feel sorry for." Christie-Ann tried a new tack. "You've cheated him over the years. Once I wouldn't have had the courage to tell you

220

that. But it's home truths time now, isn't it?"

Catherine left the room, went into the kitchen and brewed a pot of tea, which she brought back into the sitting-room. Her sister's position in the easy chair hadn't changed. Her face looked as though it had been chiselled out of granite, so hard and bitter it had become.

"I tried to end my marriage," said Catherine, almost mildly. "I thought I had made a mistake almost as soon as we'd tied the knot. I was taken with the things Edward could offer, mainly by the fact that he was better-read and better-educated than anyone I'd ever met. There was nothing wrong with Edward, really, except the one fact. He wasn't Colum."

She stopped, wondering if she had reached the point where she could tell Christie-Ann how she and Colum had renewed their love affair after the births of Clare and Lindsay. Then found that even now she couldn't. Her mouth stopped up by guilt but also by something more. The wish to keep that, the special thing, the watermark on her life, sacred to herself and Colum. It was as if by talking about it, what it represented would be dissipated. She would hang on to that as to life itself. Besides, she had no wish to wound Christie-Ann further.

"When I get away from here," said Christie-Ann, "that's the end of 'family' for me. What has 'family' ever meant but hurt and heart-break? 'The nuclear family can damage your health.' Mother's will just about broke us, didn't it? Those inplacable sulks of hers, when she tried to get her way. Maybe I married Colum to show her what I was made of. I can see what her narrow-mindedness did to you, Catherine. That, and her way of manipulating us both when we were young, withholding love unless we measured up. Families can cannibalize if you let them. Well, not me. Not any more."

"Are you going to try and find him?"

Jasmine had come home in a filthy temper and when her mother came down from her bedroom, where she had been resting, she went straight into the attack.

"Just a moment," Edward intervened. "Can't you see your mother isn't well? I must ask you to give her some consideration."

"When is she ever well?" Jasmine demanded cruelly. "Whenever anything needs facing up to, she takes to her bed. Doesn't she? Well, answer me."

"I'm not going to talk to you when you're simply spoiling for a fight."

"Pity I'm too big to be sent to my room, you mean." She shot her father a look of undisguised venom. Then, calming down with an effort, she went and sat near her mother on the large settee. Nervously Catherine plumped and re-plumped a cushion.

"Mum, don't you want to find him?"

Catherine said, in a subdued but resolute way, "The agreement was that he would become Catriona's and her husband's. For good."

Jasmine waved away the submission. "During the big catharsis, last night, you said he'd gone to London. That you'd helped him, with money. That you'd chickened out of meeting but you'd caught a glimpse of him, that once, in a restaurant. So—"

"He wanted to make his own way. He

told your grandmother that. He didn't want to see me, particularly. Or to know anything about—his father."

"But he *must*. It is only natural."

"Jasmine. Enough." Edward cut across both women, his face working. "No-one has consulted me in the matter. But let me make my position clear. Our family is you, me and your mother and I want well left alone. Is that understood?"

"You'd connive at anything, as long as it was her wish," said Jasmine, with a jealous look at Catherine. "Well, it ain't going to be the same cosy little circle here —if it ever was. I'm getting out. I'm setting up home with Kenneth Macpherson—"

"But he's your boss," said Catherine, dully.

"Yes, and he's married. And he has children. And we love each other. We've bought a flat in Byres Road and I don't really care who knows it."

"Jasmine!" her mother appealed to her. "Have you really thought about this?"

"Oh, come on, Ma. We've been through the permissive sixties. The seventies are a long way from your heyday, when the facts of life had to be concealed at all cost. Look what it did to you!"

Edward got up and shuffled over so that he stood in front of Catherine, as though protectively. He scarcely seemed to be aware of his daughter's presence.

He said directly to his wife, almost pleadingly, "Don't let her upset you. She'll come to her senses in time." To his daughter he said, with a harshness he had never before used towards her, "You are making a good job of finishing her off. And me."

Jasmine said, white-faced, but a little more penitently, "Well, you had to know some time. Kenneth and I have been seeing each other for a long time. A divorce will come through eventually. His wife just wants the money sorted out and she'll be agreeable."

Catherine moved along the settee and put her arm around her daughter.

"I wish you'd told me sooner."

"I couldn't have risked it. You'd have interfered. I couldn't have given him up."

"Well, if that's the way it's to be—"

"Catherine!" Edward's face seemed to have aged, to have grown darker and more inscrutable, almost like a stranger's. "You'll not connive at her breaking up a marriage!"

"The harm's been done, it seems." Catherine took her arm from around her daughter and let it lie in her lap. The gesture was that of resignation, a giving-up.

Jasmine got up and began to move out of the room.

"I'm sorry," she said, grimly. "When Grannie was ill, I didn't want to add to your worries. But secrets will out. We all know that, don't we, Mum? I wish you would think about Struan, I really do. Get a private detective, give him the facts."

"You heard what your father said on the matter," said Catherine stonily. "Leave it at that."

The cemetery was like the rest of Dounhead, a little broken-down but still this side of respectability. They each carried a sheaf of chrysanthemums to lay on their mother's grave, with the new headstone. Catherine placed hers which were yellow in one granite jar and said in an almost deprecatory whisper, "Graveyard flowers."

Christie-Ann's were white and she arranged them in the other vase, nodding.

"Did you ever read the Lawrence short story, *Odour of Chrysanthemums?*"

Catherine shook her head. "You should. It captures the spirit of repression in places like this, even though it's set in Nottinghamshire."

"Get you," said Catherine, with a shadow of a smile. "Reading Lawrence."

"The one I live with teaches English—did I ever tell you?—in a poly. He's very into Lawrence."

"The one you live with." Catherine stood with her arms folded, as though to warm herself. "Jasmine is going to *live* with someone. It denotes freedom of intent, doesn't it? As if you only live, or live with, if you break free of the rules."

Christie-Ann said nothing.

"I don't think things will ever be the same between Jasmine and her father," said Catherine, almost as though she were speaking to herself. "He tended to idolize her, to think everything she did was right and perfect. All this has been a terrible shock to him."

"But not to you?"

227

"Funnily enough, I'm almost glad she has the strength to kick over the traces. Properly. To say 'I love him and I'll be with him, come what may'. That's the way it should be."

"From one who knows."

"Oh yes. From one who knows." She bent again to re-arrange the flowers she had brought, then nodded towards the headstone.

"She went quickly when she went, didn't she? Almost as though she'd decided enough was enough." Almost automatically then the sisters moved towards each other and their arms went around each other. Children without a mother. "I still see her determined little figure, bent over the fire," wept Christie-Ann. "I wish she'd waited till I got here."

Catherine felt the rough wool of Christie-Ann's jacket against her mouth. Despite her own grief, she patted her sister's back comfortingly.

"Ssssh," she said. "Wheesht. Her time had come."

They drew apart almost shamefacedly and began to walk away with slow, formal steps. As they reached the cemetery gates, Christie-Ann said, "We should sell the cottage. I'll use my half for travel. I've always wanted to go to America. I hope one of the girls'll come with me."

"Not the one you live with?"

"No. I've got to find the strength to send him packing."

"You've never said whether you love him."

"I do, as a matter of fact. But what has that to do with anything? Some situations can't be allowed to go on."

"As for the cottage, I'll buy your half."

"And put him in it?"

"We'll see."

"Well, you can afford it. I can't."

9

MAYBE she had remained provincial. She was thinking over something Christie-Ann had written in a recent letter. "Dounhead's the moral equivalent of the dungheap. You should have got out of it, too, years ago. I think you would have been happier."

Her heels clattered on the college stairs and a gust of wind blew in with the laughter from two students exiting through the swing doors. Two computer students. So much had changed since she first set up the college with Mary. She had tried to keep abreast of the time, to prepare her girls for the reality of the work-place. Her students had gone on to jobs not only in Glasgow but London and abroad and some of them had done very well indeed for themselves. Provincial, yes, like herself, but it was almost like a commendation to her mind. It meant thorough, it meant professional standards. Away from the attractions of the city the girls worked harder, had fewer distractions. Here they learned a level-headedness that stood them in good stead, wherever they went later.

But provincial meant bogged down, too. That's what Christie-Ann had been trying to say. Small-town morality and hypocrisy could cramp and cripple. Maybe if she had gone away, she could have worked out a different approach to her life. She sighed. She doubted if there was all that much choice. Life laid down a pattern whether you liked it or not. Certainly for some.

In her office she sat down behind her desk and faced the decision Edward had presented her with last night. Strange considering how numb she felt, how she was still able to go through the motions of normality. She hadn't wept, she hadn't protested. Yet her husband had told her he was leaving her for another woman. The possibility had always been there, right from the start, that one of them would walk out. How had she failed to see that it could be Edward?

It was good to sit here, to be away from everybody, and just think. Not react. Just be. Sort out the genuine feelings from the false.

Was she all that sorry—or surprised? Ever since she had known about Isobel Lockhart—how he took her out for meals and away on business trips with him (and there had been those only too anxious to pass on the rumours)—she had been playing on his generosity, his sense of loyalty, yes, his decency, by her bouts of illness, the presentation of herself as someone too weak, too unprotected to be left. In some ways it was true. She did not know what she would do without the sanction of their daily lives together. He gave her the appearance of security, he had been a good father to Jasmine, he had cared for the garden, been there to talk to about college problems. Sometimes there had been bouts of genuine companionship, as when she had laid on special dinners for his business friends, or he had pulled off some coup and had been able to relate the ins and outs of it to her. Sometimes, because they had known each other for a long time, they had achieved a kind of intimacy through jokes and humour, saying through laughter what they couldn't say in so many words.

There was a poignancy about their

relationship which because they were both adult they understood and that almost equated with love on occasion. But there were great arid stretches of days when there was nothing, when each turned elsewhere for fulfilment. And Jasmine's going had changed everything. She had always been able to command her father's attention and now there was nothing between them, he was too eaten up with resentment at the man she had chosen to live with. It was strange. It was her mother Jasmine listened to now, and seemed to need, and this had somehow meant he resented Catherine too, in a way he never had before. Resent! That must have been the least of it.

Last night they had sat down to simple scrambled eggs as it was Mrs. Bendle's night off. It was one of their established routines and he had, as so often, offset the frugality of the meal by cracking a bottle of good wine.

As he'd lifted the wine to his lips he'd said, "There's something I want to discuss with you." And out it had all come, beautifully thought out, impeccably argued, spoken with detached gentleness in true Edward fashion.

"Isobel feels we have to start a family now or never. Her child-bearing days will soon be over. It doesn't matter to me but it does to her and I suppose I would like a son."

Chickens home to roost.

She hadn't a leg to stand on. No recriminations to make. He was the one who had made the marriage work, who had stayed with her when she had openly invited him to go.

The secret of Struan coming out in the family, that too had had its effect. Once Jasmine had given up her pleas to try and track him down, he had asked Catherine what her true wishes were. But she had refused to talk about them. He was not to know about the pain. But it must have rankled. Why else would he say now he had always wanted a son? If anything hurt now, that did, but only as a resonance of the much larger pain that was Struan.

He was going to take early retirement. Look for a villa in Spain. Improve his golf. Life should be about more than earning money and he was fed-up with jet-lag, he wanted Candide-like to cultivate his garden.

"The thing is, Catherine, I do want a divorce."

She had thought she was hearing things. But he had been considerate even there. It would have been too messy before, but now it could take place when they had been separated for a couple of years and the sooner that separation took place the better, so he was going to move out. To a rented flat in Glasgow in the first place until he and Isobel found what they wanted. He thought they could be happy. She was a girl of great sensitivity and their feelings for each other had stood the test of time.

A bit like Jasmine and Kenneth in reverse. It was almost comical when you thought about it. No more than she deserved, though. She could hear her late mother's words very clearly in her mind, delivered with a Presbyterian harshness that was almost relish: *As ye sow, so shall ye reap.*

And then had come the point where she answered. This calm, rational person had matched his pleas with understanding

235

generosity. Yes, of course, he could have his divorce. Of course, she would not stand in his way. They had both known the marriage was only tied together with string, maybe not even that, but cheap raffia straw, and she hoped he and Isobel would be able to find happiness and have the son they both wanted.

She had risen and taken the dishes from the table and washed them by hand because there were not enough to justify the machine and she had become quite energy-conscious. She had put everything back in its place in the spotless modern kitchen and hung up the dish-towel folded once, neatly, corner to corner.

Then she had gone back in and taken out her cross-stitch embroidery and turned on the television for him so that he could watch the news as always.

"Catherine," he had said. "You are very quiet. I am sorry if I have shocked you."

And she had responded, very civilly, "What is there to say?"

"You can visit your paramour in the cottage when I'm gone, as often as you like."

She had felt cold and numb before that

but suddenly she was sinking through new depths of chill, the defences of her body attacked as though she were going down with influenza. She had shaken, her very teeth had chattered, the embroidery had fallen useless into her lap.

A voice, her own it appeared, was saying "He isn't my paramour. How dare you say that? The man is an invalid."

"You didn't think to consult me about the cottage, did you?"

"You were too busy. You were finishing the Inverclad deal."

"It didn't occur to you in any case that I should be consulted."

"The cottage was left to Christie-Ann and me. She needed the money so I bought her out. I don't want to sell the cottage so why shouldn't I rent it to a friend?"

"You'll see no rent from him!"

"Does it matter? You forget what the war did to him. He didn't have a lucky war as you had."

"You should have known what was happening to Jasmine. Why did she never confide in you?"

She hadn't known what to say to him. It

was as though he was somehow defending himself, because he wanted to leave her, by dragging out every count he could think of against her. In the end, she had walked out of the room while the rage and resentment were still vibrating between them. They had never rowed like this in their whole married life and therefore there were no ground rules to go by. The pain and the hurt had been devastating.

She put her head on her hand now and sighed. A small, pitiable sound. The cold feeling was returning, she began to shake once again. She poured some water from a carafe and drank it. Then she shrugged on her coat. She wasn't sure whether there was a class she should be taking. Let it take care of itself.

She had taken a tranquillizer before catching the train and now with the somewhat greasy coffee she took another. She didn't much care for the veil of apathetic unreality they lowered between her and existence, but she hoped she might relax enough to sleep.

"Maybe staying with Christie-Ann would be a good idea," Edward had said.

Not that she had allowed him to say much. "Just get out. Go," she had reiterated. "I want to know you will be all right." This last was from him. She could not really fault him. She just wanted him not to be there any more. But he had taken his time, methodical and fair about what he could take with him. Then one morning she had got up and he was gone and her life was a new blank page with nothing written on it. So she had caught the train to Euston but without letting Christie-Ann know in advance. She did not even know whether she would be welcome.

London was a charivari of sound and distractions. Such a variety of nations and colours, from the flash of saris to the bright cotton of African robes. So many ways of dressing, of behaving. I don't have the primer for this, she thought, Dounhead and its known ways suddenly infinitely desirable. But she pressed on, won a taxi and took it to Christie-Ann's West London flat. It was in a small block next to council high-rise flats, but backing on to a park. The lover, she knew, was still there, had not yet been given his marching orders.

Christie-Ann's reaction when she answered her ring was almost comical.

"Catherine! What—why—?"

"I've come," she said, clearly, although she had not acknowledged it to herself even, till then, "to look for Struan."

For some reason, Christie-Ann looked down at the hand gripping the soft-topped suitcase and took in the knuckles, strained and white.

"Then you'd better come in," she said softly. "But I wish I'd known you were coming."

"What made you suddenly determined to find Struan again?" Lindsay demanded.

They had eaten, a picky meal of bean-sprouts and humous and now they sat about the flat like characters in a play, every eye focused relentlessly on the one they obviously considered the lead player: Catherine.

She was dishevelled and talkative, following Christie-Ann into the kitchen to make a point, unfolding the bitter catalogue of her life, the separation from Edward, with a thoroughness that would not have disgraced the recording angel.

Recounting what had happened the day they took Struan away from her, when he was twenty-four hours old. Making them understand how she had felt that day in Glasgow, when she could have spoken to him, when dread and desire had warred in her to such an extent that she had literally been unable to act, to speak, to do anything. How much she had regretted it afterwards and yet the dread had still to be fought. Of what he would think of her, how he might reproach her. As he had every right to do.

She took a cigarette from Don, Christie-Ann's live-in-man who looked gratifyingly like his idol, Lawrence, with a dark beard and piercing eyes, though the effect was slightly offset by scruffy jeans and large grubby tennis shoes. She was not used to wine and her gestures were becoming more extravagant.

"See?" she begged them. "Since Edward went I feel a bit like a butterfly coming out of the chrysalis. You would think that would be a pleasant experience, wouldn't you?"—she appealed to Lindsay, who sat with her knees under her, tensely attentive—"but I'm here to tell you it

241

hurts. You know you've got to evolve into something different from what you have been all your life, but you've been cocooned. You've been making money, you've been making a position for yourself in the community, you know the man you have isn't right for you yet habit has its charms and you've got a daughter you both love. You make up to yourself for the deficiencies in your emotional life. You say 'I'll treat myself to a new Rover, in that classy, near-black greeny colour.' Or you think 'I'll get the house done up again.' It's what I mean by a cocoon—you cocoon yourself, you shut out the hurts and you lose touch with who you really are."

"You have a lot of self-knowledge," said Don, in his cool tutor's way.

"Much good it's done me. All I know is that when I reach a low ebb in my life, what comes through is a kind of blind need to get my baby back, to go back to the beginning and *not* give him away." She almost threw down the cigarette butt and the tears Christie-Ann had waited for all evening, with a kind of shaky calm, began in a tideless flood. Nothing they could say made any difference. Catherine walked up and down the room, sobbing into a handkerchief provided by Don, disappearing into the bathroom, emerging dry-eyed only to start again.

At last Christie-Ann said, on a note of exhausted and by now astringent patience, "I think you should go to your bed. I'll bring you some hot milk. We'll talk in the morning." She looked at Don. "Thank God it's Saturday."

"What was the name of his adoptive parents?" said Lindsay. "We'll go through the names in the phone book, for a start."

"Maclennan. But he took the name Brodie when he came to London. He thought it sounded better for an actor."

"One thing's for sure," said Lindsay. "He hasn't hit the bigtime. Struan Brodie is not a name I've seen on any hoardings."

"No, but he could be a bit player, a character actor, making a living," Christie-Ann interjected.

"He's probably clerking in Bloomsbury," said Don.

"Wait a minute!" Lindsay held up an imperative hand. "There's an S. Brodie, twelve Alkington Gardens, S.W. four-teen—"

"Oh, God," said Catherine, holding a hand to her chest. "Do you think it's him?"

"Just do it," said Lindsay. "Take a deep breath, pick up the phone, and dial."

"What do I say?"

"Just say: 'Is that Struan Brodie? Well this is a long-lost relative of yours, who happens to be in London'—"

"Not say straight away I'm his mother?"

"Put it any way you like. But do it." Lindsay held out the receiver.

In the end a woman's voice, light and curious, had answered and after some awkward word-play had handed her on to Struan. His voice had sounded flattened, deliberately ironed out of all emotion. But at least he had agreed to see her. She had offered to take him to lunch, anywhere he liked, but he had said, "No, come over here," and she had acquiesced, too scared and humble to ask if she could bring someone with her.

When he opened the door, she almost smiled, because it was there, the dark quiff that made him look like Colum. He was lean, sharp-eyed, very much in the laid-back seventies mode with his corduroy jeans and dark navy pullover. The flat was light, there was that to be said for it, but sparsely furnished to the point of bareness, neutral except for some contemporary prints, a Davie and a Hoyland on the wall.

"Well, well, well," he said and his voice was carefully modulated and still carried some of the lilting West Highland intonation. "Fancy after all these years." He held out his hand and she took it, words dying in her throat. She looked round for the girl with the questioning voice. "No," he said, interpreting her thoughts, "Barbara thought it best to make herself scarce. Leave the scene bare for the primal drama as it were." He chuckled, rocking back on his white tennis shoes. Why did they all wear these abominations, as though they had bad feet or no money for anything better?

"Come in, Catherine," he said. "You don't mind me calling you Catherine? Mother seems a bit superfluous. Do they call you the full Catherine, or Kate or Kitty or something like that?"

She sat down and ran her tongue along dry lips, "I've always been the full Catherine. Not Cather-een, Catherine to rhyme with brine." She managed a smile. On the level, it was just social, it wasn't hard, he looked quite relaxed and welcoming.

"Coffee?"

"In a bit," she pleaded. "Let me look at you first." He stood in front of her, hands in pockets, still rocking, his expression one of cultivated amused detachment.

"Am I up to expectations?"

"You're so like your father," she said helplessly.

"Is that good?"

"Oh, yes. Good."

"He put it about a bit, though. Married your sister, my technical aunt, didn't he? How many did he have by her?"

"Two girls." She wanted him to stop the hectoring. She was sure that was what he was up to. She looked down at her hands and couldn't see them for tears. She took a deep breath. "But tell me about you first. You wanted to be an actor, didn't you? Did it happen?"

He laughed. "No way. I hadn't enough talent to fill a thimble. No. What I do now is teach actors how to relax. A special technique, to do with alignment of the spine and head. I could teach you. You look as though you might get quite tense. Do you?"

She nodded, the tears miraculously liquidated. If he was going to teach her to relax, that might mean he wanted to go on seeing her. A kind of mad pleasure pervaded her. She felt radiant. She threw off her coat.

"I'm sure you were fine as an actor."

"I'm more into therapeutic techniques now. Barbara, she's a therapist for people with sexual and marital problems. You see, I had a thorny patch, when I discovered Scotland's gift to stage and screen was getting flung back in Scotland's face. 'Eneugh!' Folk were saying. 'This tripe, this sheep's entrails, this turnip-head from the Boondocks, *this* is all you have to offer? Keep it. Take it back.' Only I wouldn't go back. My Mother and Father —saving the expression, but you know who I mean—they would have been glad to see me crawling back over Carter Bar. They would have wiped the snot from my face and stood me on my feet and pointed me in the right direction. *Their* direction.

"So I have been into therapy myself. I've *been* there. I discovered one thing, Catherine, and I have to tell you, though I don't say it with any intention of upsetting you. I discovered I hated you. You got the blame for all my troubles. That's what happens to mothers, even conventional ones who don't hand you over to someone else at birth. You hadn't even been able to bring yourself to talk to me that day in Glasgow and you can't imagine how often I'd set up the scenario for that. You've got to be rejected by your *mother*, for Christ's sake, before you know what rejection feels like. It was my turn for the big rejection trip and I rejected you over and over again. I hated you. I still hate you, I think, but that's my bag. With Barbara's help, I hope I've put the past behind me. Grown up." Then he smiled, dispassionately.

"Well, if you hate me, it's no more than I deserve." It was worse than she had ever anticipated, the raw pain. It was no act he was putting on. The suffering he had gone through was patent now, in the way his angular body seemed to tighten in on itself, the way his fists went to his mouth for the nails to be bitten. A harrowing and harrowed expression darkened his features. She pleaded to the Deity for the courage to move nearer to him on the settee, to touch him, take one of those balled fists in her hand and loosen the fingers, but it was too much to ask, she could not accord herself the privilege. They stared at each other. "I wish I had made the move sooner," she said. "I know it's all too late, but I would like you to know there hasn't been a day in my life when I haven't thought of you. So I've paid, too. I've paid my dues. In suffering."

He moved his shoulders back, loosened the unconsciously balled fists, shook out his arms and seemed to uncoil and relax once more before her eyes. "Get me," he said. "At least I know how to cope with physical tensions. Ease your shoulders, Catherine. Relax those hands. You could take that coffee now?"

"Yes, please."

When he came back with two mugs with the spoons standing up in them and a variety of small biscuits on a large plate, she gazed up at him and said, "Do you want to know about your father?"

"He's not been in the picture," he said. "I don't know why that should be. You were always the more substantial shadow."

"He's been very ill. He was wounded in the war and they didn't get all the shrapnel out at the time."

"Am I like him? I don't think I'm very like you."

"You have his head. His hair. His hands."

"You married someone else. Do you still see him?"

"My marriage is finished. So is his, virtually. My sister has lived in London for twenty years."

"I don't know if I'm entitled to ask this. But do you still have any feelings for him, my father, I mean?"

"Yes, I do." It came out very straightforwardly, but softly.

"Crumbs," he said. "What a dog's breakfast."

"Yes," she admitted.

He unfolded his long body, put down the mug and paced with long, lithe steps up and down the room.

"I have to make it clear, Catherine, this meeting is a one-off. Barbara says I should keep it open-ended, but what I said about how I feel towards you is the truth and I don't think I can handle a coy, *let's forget it all and get together* situation. You've satisfied your curiosity about how I look and I've put a face to my object of hatred . . ."

"Don't get upset," she pleaded. She opened the catch on her brown leather handbag and took out a long buff envelope, holding it out towards him. "I didn't come here to upset you."

"No. I realize that. We're both trying hard to do the civilized thing. I know that."

She shook the envelope like a fan, directing his attention towards it.

"What's this?"

"Are you and—Barbara married or living together?"

"Living with each other."

"Well, you've probably got a mortgage

on the flat, or you might want a bigger one. Whatever. I'm an independent woman, financially, I've worked all my days, it's been my salvation. Your sister Jasmine has had her share over the years. That's yours. It's a cheque for ten thousand pounds."

"I can't take conscience money. You must see that." He handed her back the envelope, unopened, as though it might burn his fingers.

She put it down on the scratched coffee table. "Take it. I'll find one way or another of giving it to you." He turned deliberately away from her, ignoring the look of entreaty on her face.

"Don't do this to me," he pleaded.

She rose, stiffly, pulling her good camel coat that he had never invited her to take off around her and arranging the tie belt fastidiously.

"You might feel differently about seeing me again," she said, her voice thick. "And when you do—"

"I don't mean any gratuitous hurt," he said, with a cold reasonableness, "but we've got to function within our psychological limits. Just as you did all these years when you couldn't see me."

"Oh, Struan," she said and blundered towards him. He held out his hand like a lance.

"This is goodbye." He made a little pantomime of it, rising up and down on his toes, raising his eyebrows, grimacing. "Take care of yourself, Catherine."

"You too."

"And regards to my Dad."

She was halfway towards the taxi rank before she realized he had somehow stuffed the unopened buff envelope into the open side compartment of her handbag.

"I liked him," she said to Christie-Ann. "I felt he was someone to be proud of. He wasn't vindictive, just honest."

"What will you do now?"

"Go back. Face the jackals. 'See her. Her man left her'."

"It won't be that bad."

"Oh, yes, it will be. Bad as can be."

Christie-Ann moved restlessly on the settee, rearranging her jean-clad legs which had been tucked up under her. She looked pale. Her blonded hair, which she had arranged in one of the fashionable fuzzy perms, looked as though it had not yet been combed. A tight, washed-in jumper with a low neck revealed cleavage. In a maddening way, thought Catherine, she looked her best, her most delectable, when she was ungroomed.

"Wait a day or two," she pleaded.

"I can't see the sense of putting it off. I've got to get back to the college and you've run out of days off."

"He might change his mind. Get in touch."

"Don't," said Catherine, abruptly. "I won't delude myself. His decision was fair and I'll abide by it."

"Even if it kills you." Christie-Ann looked at her evenly. "That's you, isn't it? You stuck to Edward all these years, even if it killed you. I could go and see Struan—"

"No!"

"Why not?"

"It would be harassment. We've no rights in the matter—"

"But you're on your own, you need some support—"

254

"Oh, come on, Christie-Ann. The normal family rules don't apply."

"OK. Well, stay on because I want you to."

"You don't need me. You've got Don, and Lindsay popping in all the time."

Christie-Ann brushed imaginary creases from the knee of her jeans. "Well, that's it. I want you to be around when I tell Don he has to go."

"You mean it?"

"We can't go on as we are."

When he came in from college, the first thing Don did was put his arms around Christie-Ann and kiss her.

"What's for supper? Want me to go down the Chinese chippy?" He used the vernacular with the happy unconscious abandon of one of his students.

"No. I'm doing chicken and veg in the wok."

"Goody. I'm starving." He kissed her again then turned to Catherine. "Hi. Had a good day?"

"We've done nothing but talk," said Catherine.

"About Struan?"

"No." Christie-Ann had gone into the kitchen to start work on the meal and was out of earshot. "Funnily enough, about you. You and Christie-Ann."

His instant wariness was almost comic.

"I'm not sure I like that. Our emotional life isn't public property."

"No, but Christie-Ann needs somebody to talk to. She's very worried about the difference in your ages—"

"Totally irrelevant. For God's sake this is cosmopolitan London, it isn't the age of Jane Austen."

"It's not irrelevant to her. However it may seem to the contrary, Don, we're very conventional people. Christie-Ann would rather be married than living in what our mother would have called sin." She tried to keep it light and bantering but that was not how it came out.

"Let her get a divorce, then, and I'll marry her. No problem." He rose and threw wide the kitchen door, bawling at Christie-Ann. "Have you been talking about our intimate life with her? The problems are between you and me. Nothing to do with your sister."

Catherine stood up, flustered. "God, I didn't mean to start anything."

"No. Good job you did." Don's face had gone very red. He had taken off his bomber jacket and now he rolled up his shirt sleeves as he rummaged in a kitchen drawer for cutlery to set the table, his face only inches from Christie-Ann's set one and the spitting, hissing wok.

"I told Catherine I want you to leave," Christie-Ann shouted. "If you want wine there's a Liebfraumilch in the fridge."

Don threw the cutlery down in front of Catherine. "Lay that," he ordered. She meekly obeyed.

"Did you tell Catherine how we made love last night?"

"Donald, don't go over the top."

"It's relevant. You've been telling me to go practically ever since I arrived, but it all gets unsaid when we go to bed. Doesn't it? You little whore."

Catherine stood helplessly by the window of the sitting-room, spoons for dessert still in her hand, embarrassment paralyzing her limbs and something more, a sad, echoing sexual envy rolling through her mind in waves. Down below in the

257

street she saw Jamaican teenagers, boys, progress towards the local disco as though they already heard the music, their steps half-dancing, carefree, uninhibited, saying something about the enjoyment, the celebration, of life that she had forgotten. She was no vehicle for joy, she, whose hips were spreading, whose hair was greying, whose marriage had been set aside.

"Sit down." Don came in from the kitchen, carrying warmed plates. "You started this. We were happy as pigs in muck till you came down with your Presbyterian ways. Christie-Ann's told me how the pair of you were brought up. Well, grown-up people do something about their useless inhibitions. Calvin's dead. You don't have to appear before the congregation and confess your sins any more. The congregation's too busy, out there sinning on its own."

"Don't pick on Catherine." Christie-Ann carried a large dish of steaming rice, chicken and vegetables and moved the soy sauce from sideboard to table. They began eating absent-mindedly. Christie-Ann said bleakly, "I've had one husband. What do I want with another?" Tears ran down her

258

face and she wiped them away with the heel of her palm. Catherine's embarrassment, her sense almost of voyeurism, increased. Desperately she concentrated on her food, distinguishing spring onions, sweetcorn, the crunch of celery.

"This tastes nice," she volunteered.

"Sweetheart," Don said to Christie-Ann, "don't cry." Catherine might as well not have been there. "I know what a disaster it was, the first time. That's because it wasn't a real marriage. This time it is. We're married already. All it needs is a piece of paper."

"I should have more sense." Christie-Ann wept bitterly. "I should have enough sense for both of us."

"What's sense got to do with it?"

"Everything, everything. I've no guarantee I won't be left a lonely old woman, while you go off to seminars chasing youthful bits of skirt."

He laughed then. Poured himself some more wine and laughed, as though he just won some hard-fought ground. Catherine looked up from her food, finding something about Christie-Ann's choice of words

almost comic, too. Her smile was woe-
begone.

"There's no guarantee about anything
lasting, Christie-Ann," she found herself
saying.

"There! You see!"

"Do you think I should marry him
then?" Christie-Ann demanded of her
sister, incredulously.

"Do you love him?"

There was a silence, while Don's hand
stopped in mid-gesture as it lifted the wine
glass to his lips.

"I'll never get over the embarrassment."

"But 'Do you love him?'" Remorse-
lessly, Don parodied Catherine.

He wasn't very clever, Christie-Ann had
told Catherine. He didn't pass exams
easily. But he had a doggedness in his
character and an openness that had made
her feel he was one of those men who
would go on growing. Who would get
there in the end. He had been brought up
by strangers, a virtual orphan from the age
of six.

"I'm not going to say it." Christie-Ann
shook her head from side to side.

"Please say it," he said, quietly.

"I suppose I do."

It wasn't relevant, Catherine thought, as she sipped her coffee and watched them huddle together on the sofa like two waifs from a storm, but Christie-Ann did have a son. Not like me, who had one and lost him.

10

WHAT *will folk think?* The words had always been woven like a lumpy strand throughout her mother's existence, and now going home from London on the train she felt the same familiar, uncomfortable sense of something out of kilter, something not right when you went against the common grain.

They would have had a field day in Dounhead over Edward's decamping and in the main sympathies would not have been with her, because of her success with the college and the fact that she was mistress of one of the best-kept houses in Hawktoun Road. She knew that the gossips in Dounhead (and who wasn't a gossip there?—living in a small town gave automatic qualification) had always regarded her as a bit of a snob and *arriviste*, given to putting on unjustifiable airs. Edward's English accent had put both of them beyond the pale and would have done the same for Jasmine had she not

262

aggressively adopted the local *patois*. The consensus would be that she had got no more than her comeuppance. She would know it every time she went into a shop or signed on a student from the lower bourgeoisie. Worst of all would be the false expressions of sympathy dished out by those who in their private enclaves would most greatly rejoice.

She felt a sense of quavering vulnerability, but she wasn't going to back down because of it. She was going to remain head of the college and put her plans for expansion on the computer side into action. She wasn't going to move out of the big house, either. One day Jasmine would marry Kenneth Macpherson, after his messy divorce went through and there might be grandchildren who would play in a sandpit in the garden. Pray God! Though she feared Jasmine would be more certain and sure a mother than she had been.

She wobbled through to the buffet car and came back with the usual unpalatable-looking BR coffee, thinking of her own mother, as she often did, and the unquantifiable influences she had had on her life. How strong she had been. They would not have survived but for that strength, especially after her father had died, but that very strength had somehow put everything else out of balance.

So much else had gone by the board, in that struggle for life and some kind of dignity. There hadn't been much kindness, much compassion. Sometimes she thought this applied to Scotland, right across the board. It had suffered too much, too many partings, too unforgiving a kirk, too harsh an economy, too selfish a neighbour and partner in England, and this had caused a stunting, a lack of generosity in the spirit. But that could be all nonsense, a rationalization of her own sense of deprivation. Her mother had used threats and dire warnings to train her up in the way she wanted her to go. Her mother had convinced her you were not good or love-worthy until you had fulfilled the last parental and then the last neighbourhood criterion. It had only been in her later adult life, that she had found there was a God who could love you despite your failings. That had been a revelation indeed, the cornerstone of her adult identity and it was that which had made it possible for her to get on the train, to come back. *What will folk think?* She finished her coffee and let her mother's harassed, hungry, worried images fade from her mind. Folk, the feared other, were only mirror-images of yourself, who had not yet learned that life is lived by kindness and forgiveness. *Lie down, little mother. Lie down.*

Of Edward she had scarcely allowed herself to think anything from the day he had left. Now as the train cut its great rhythmic swathe through the heart of Midland England, she examined the shabby ragbag of faded, guilty emotions which she had felt towards him for years.

There had been a man worth loving there but she had consistently turned her face away from him and so had never known him. Instead she had known an Edward pedantic in scholarship, obsessive in his interests, like gardening and opera, acerbic and sometimes hurtful in wit. She had made him what he was. She acknowledged that. She had made him into the man who had been able to tell her of his departure with something like vengeance and even hatred in his expression. Yes, she

265

had done that. He was better off without her and she would get used to the garden without that spare, obsessive figure with its wounded look haunting greenhouse and summerhouse. She acknowledged, however, that the shock of his going was still with her and would be for a long time to come. Habit, even the habit of a failed, sad marriage, died hard.

Uneasily, because now she was getting closer to the reality of what her life would be like, without Edward and without Jasmine, she stirred in her seat. She opened her handbag and sorted aimlessly through the contents, coming to the last letter she'd had from her old friend Mary Mackinnon. What was it Mary had said to her before she had left all these years before to marry her New England love? "I can never see you moving away from Dounhead, Catherine. You're everything good and Scottish and reliable." She'd certainly been right about the first part. She would never leave Dounhead now. She looked at the snapshot Mary had enclosed with the letter. It showed a slender, blonde woman laughing into the sun, ageless and pretty, bearing hardly any

266

resemblance to the solid, tweedy girl who had emigrated. Christie-Ann, too, had uncovered this skill, in common with a lot of women, of standing age on its head, of looking younger in middle-age than they ever had as twenty-year olds. If there was some secret, she herself had been too busy or bruised to find it. Or too locked in the past, unable to shake off its strictures. Whatever. She did not feel as young as her daughter, but as old as her mother. She would not change now.

"Will you go and see Colum for me?" Christie-Ann had begged. "I can't write to him and ask for a divorce."

"Why ever not?"

"Because—of the way he is."

"Christie-Ann," she had protested weakly. "it is something you should do yourself."

"You're closer to him than me. Go and see him at the cottage and broach the subject sideways, as it were. I don't want it to be too great a shock. You could say something like 'How would you feel if Christie-Ann wanted to marry again?' keeping it all very hypothetical and then, depending on his response, you could say something like 'I feel she may want to, one day. Marry again, I mean'."

She had laughed, in the end, at the pussyfooting and vacillation which Christie-Ann had swathed around her old Calvinistic guilts, but she was suffering the same guilts, be it vicariously, as she walked now towards the cottage to see Colum for the first time since her return home.

For almost a week she had been catching up at the college, learning to ignore the looks and nudges and sly examinations of her expression. Did they think she would have "Rejected" stamped all over her? She had been brisk, business-like and effective and at home she had reorganized rooms, moving her own bedroom to the front of the house so that she could hear night traffic, voices, the hum of existence. Sometimes, at breakfast or working on her petit point, she had wept.

She had met Lucille in the street and learned from her that Colum knew about Edward leaving. Although she had quite a large brood of her own, not all of them grown-up or left home, Lucille called on her brother daily, making sure he ate properly, that there was nothing he needed. She had been fulsome in her gratitude over the cottage, saying it was ideal for Colum, with its wide, old doors and paved yard, because he still had to spend a large part of the day in his wheelchair.

He was sitting in his wheelchair by the window when she went in and deliberately moved himself so that he could take her hand before he let her sit down opposite him. He held and squeezed her hand then raised it to his lips and even then did not let go, but drew her towards him so that his face was pressed against the breast of her coat. She stood for a moment, moved and reassured and absurdly happy and at home. For a moment. It couldn't last because there was a lot to talk about.

"Are you all right?" he asked roughly. "You shouldn't have taken off like that, leaving your friends worried about you."

"I couldn't face the so-called sympathy," she admitted.

"Well, now you're here, take off your coat. Shall I make you a cup of tea?"

"No, let me."

"I can manage fine," he said. "And you mustn't mollycoddle me." He swept past her into the tiny kitchenette, filled a light aluminium kettle at the sink and set it on the low gas cooker to boil. "No problem!" He spread his hands wide and grinned at her. "Independence is what you long for, while you're in hospital, you know. And that's what you and Christie-Ann have given me here. And I can tell you, I'm bloody grateful."

"Christie-Ann wants a divorce." Of course it wasn't the way she had meant to bring it up, but somehow there was no holding it back. "Seems like it's in the air, Colum. First Edward . . ."

She carried the mugs of tea back into the sitting-room and he followed on with a packet of biscuits. "She lives with this person, Don, he's a good bit younger than she is, but he's a nice man, I got to know him—"

"Sit down," he ordered, "and start at the beginning."

She took a sip of the tea and could feel a light sweat break out on her brow.

"She asked me to bring it up with you, because she didn't know how to write to you about it. She's full of guilts and indecisions but she does seem fond of Don and they've made a decent life together."

"She can have a divorce, for all I care." She felt the tears rise quickly at the brusque, cutting edge to his voice. "We should have done it years ago, it would have been far more honest."

"Well, there were the girls to consider," she said quietly, "and they are fond of you both."

"They've turned out all right, haven't they?" He looked at her heavy-eyed. "No thanks to me. All the credit has to go to her. Their mother."

"They're fine." Suddenly she was too tired to utter another word. She wanted to tell Colum about seeing Struan but it seemed to demand more strength of will than she had at her command. She looked round the little room. Lucille and her husband had laid fitted whipcord carpeting, which made it easier for the wheelchair. In the old days her mother had had patchy linoleum and hand-made rag rugs. The lino had been polished to within an inch of its life and the rugs had been shaken twice a day. Only the old steel range was the same. She was glad of that.

She suddenly wondered what Struan would make of this place. Not just the cottage, but Dounhead. And of his father. "Give my regards to my dad", he had said, burning with pride and irony and hatred. Nor had he taken the money, the Judas money as he saw it, but the money with which she had hoped to purchase a small bit of peace of mind.

Colum was looking at her closely. "You've something else to tell me, haven't you?" He had always had this uncanny knack of knowing what went on in her mind.

"I don't know if I should. You've had enough upset for one day."

"Go on. Spill the beans."

"I saw our son. I saw Struan."

He spun his chair round and forward so that they were almost face to face. She saw anger and a certain bewilderment over the proposed divorce give way to something more primitive—to surprise and joy and a terrible need to know.

"You never told me this. That you intended to try and see him."

"I didn't know what was in the back of my mind till I got to London. I was all mixed up because Edward had upped and left so unexpectedly. It—it really jolted me, made me see what was important. And the most important thing, almost from the day I gave him up, was our baby."

She did not cry, but gave him such a look of luminous pain he moved forward again and held both of her hands. She let her head rest on his shoulder and said quaveringly, "Wrong turnings, Colum. We make wrong turnings and giving the baby up was mine. But never a day has passed that I haven't thought of him."

"Poor love." He hooked her chin up with his forefinger and a look of naked honesty passed between them. "I never meant to do that to you. But you saw him? What was he like? Will you see him again?"

She shook her head.

"I can't talk about it."

"What do you mean, you can't talk about it?"

"It's just too painful. He—he let me see him the once, but he has no wish to continue the relationship. I—I wanted to give him some money—"

"You shouldn't have done that, Catherine."

"Well, maybe not. But I wanted to make up for some of the things he'd gone without."

"But he would have his pride."

"Yes."

"Who was he like?"

"You more than me. His hair grows the same way as yours. He's not as broad as you, but he's taller. And he had a nice smile."

"Is he married?"

"He has a girl called Barbara. And he teaches a system of posture and relaxation."

"Well, he could have turned out a crook or a thug. Be grateful."

"I am. I think he's a nice man."

There were no words to cover what they both felt then. And so there was only silence between them, till she rose to go.

She had not thought the divorce from Edward would hurt so much. It was as though the years of convincing herself he did not matter to her were suddenly upended and a whole new set of lost possibilities confronted her. What if she had tried harder, paid less attention to her work, joined in some of his interests and enthusiasms?

Something better and warmer might have resulted. He had always held out the hope. There was a good deal of guilt in what she felt, for she had been the one who closed doors and erected barriers. She could even have talked to him more about Struan. He would have understood. He was neither a hard man nor a cold one.

Perhaps it was this distaste for herself that prevented her from going to Christie-Ann's and Don's wedding. She had no wish to examine her part in this other divorce. The complexity of life confounded her and really, as though in atonement, she wanted to keep her present life simple and ordered. She wanted to keep away from London because that was where Struan was and Struan wanted nothing to do with her.

Christie-Ann and Don had a register office marriage attended by the girls Clare and Lindsay, Lindsay's husband and a few friends. They sent Catherine cards from Martinique where they went on honeymoon. She saw the same cards on Colum's mantelpiece. Presumably this was going to be regarded as a thoroughly modern divorce, with no offence meant and none taken. She could not fathom how Colum felt about it all, except that she detected in his responses some of her own regret and bewilderment and eventually a certain relief.

The week before he was due in hospital for yet another operation, she took Colum out in her car for a spring picnic. They saw each other once or twice a week and she knew tongues wagged about them, but they had decided to let things take their course. They needed to see each other, to talk about the people who were important to them.

Since starting to live at the cottage, Colum had become a kind of local ombudsman and he was talking now of standing for the council. It went without saying that because of long periods of enforced rest he was well-read, well-informed about the matters that concerned local people, but it was his nature, non-judgemental and compassionate, that drew them to him. It meant, nonetheless, that he lived in a kind of perpetual stir and the house was already silting up with official handouts and forms and with reference books and pamphlets, and visited by anxious-looking citizens at all hours of the day and night.

The book that had been mooted in hospital had been put, temporarily, or at least so Colum claimed, on the back burner. Catherine saw that real life was more important to him than fictional ones and doubted now if the Great Work, as Colum referred to it with increasing facetiousness, would ever see the light of day.

Although both of Colum's parents were now dead, and the family, save for Lucille, well scattered, something of the raffishness of the old Brodie ménage clung to Colum's new residence. He still gambled, though lightly so that disreputable cronies discussing the merits of the 3.30 at Aintree, or seeking a sub, mingled with ex-patient friends calling for a chat, the minister dropping by with a book or someone wanting help with a claim for a disablement allowance.

She drove him away from Lanarkshire

and its grey little towns towards the bright spring sunshine of the Trossachs. He was in some pain whenever he moved but they got out of the car by the lochside and with her help he struggled over a grassy bank to share a rug with her on a fallen tree trunk. She brought out fresh baps spread with tongue and mustard or hard-boiled eggs with cress and poured scalding coffee from a business-like flask.

"This is the life." She could see in the harsh sunlight how a winter of pain had etched lines on his face and taken the colour from it, yet he smiled at her with the same big, generous smile that had enchanted her when she was seventeen and still had the power to do so.

She shivered a little and tied the woollen scarf around her neck a little more tightly. "It's good when it's just the two of us," she acknowledged. "I hate having to share you with those—hangers-on." He said nothing, merely bit into his roll and looked round at the sparkling scene. "You could come and live with me in Hawktoun Road. After the operation. I would look after you." She had not meant to say any of

278

this, and was aware of the roll swelling dryly in her mouth as she looked at him.

At last, he extended an arm, indicating she should move closer and he drew her into his side so that her head snuggled on his shoulder.

"Could you come and live in the cottage, with me?"

"No!" It burst from her with involuntary vehemence. "I—I would have to have some sort of order, Colum. I couldn't exist with those piles of papers and the doorbell going every five minutes." The strength of her denial reverberated between them and drove them apart, aghast.

"Well, no more could I live among the touch-me-nots of Hawktoun Road. The front grass there looks as though someone's manicured it with a pair of scissors—"

"I don't deny I like nice things. My pictures, my stereo, my books, are my consolation. Edward taught me to enjoy them."

"I prefer humanity to things."

"*You* enjoy books."

"I don't need to own them to enjoy them."

"I do."

"That's the difference between us."

She began to laugh then.

"You know, the same things apply that applied when I first knew you. I don't like your life-style and yet—"

"Go on. Say it."

"And yet I love you." Her voice tailed off.

His gaze met hers then turned a shade bleakly towards the slapping waters of the loch.

"You know the outcome of this new operation is imponderable? Ostensibly it's to get me on my feet again but I've seen the surgeon's face when he talks to me about it—I feel it's just another shot in the dark."

"It doesn't matter to me," she said, wildly. "Whether you walk or not."

He said in a controlled, even voice, "Let's take each day as it comes. The moment, after all, is all we have. We've got now, we've got a picnic, we've got guests, even." He threw the remainder of a bap to some hopeful birds fluttering nearby. "Whether we live together or apart, we've got each other, haven't we?"

While she waited to ring the hospital to ask how he was after the operation, the doorbell rang. She ran down to answer it, thinking it might be Lucille to invite her to go with her at visiting time. Jasmine stood there, wearing her expensive Burberry and highly polished chestnut brown leather boots, a fine leather suitcase at her feet.

Her arms opened automatically. "Jasmine! I didn't expect—"

"I've left him," said Jasmine. "Oh, Mum, let me in before I make a fool of myself."

They both made towards the kitchen rather than the formality of the sitting-room. This was where Jasmine had had her supper as a little girl, waiting for her mother and father to come home. Catherine looked at her daughter now, seeing so much of Edward's English reserve in that face and yet some of her own volatility.

"What happened?" She took Jasmine's coat from her and hung it on the hook behind the door that had once held her childish garments. Her eyes smarted.

"You know Douglas, the youngest of Ken's children? They've found out he's got a heart condition, he's going to need a lot of treatment and care. Ken's always adored that child. It was Douglas who made it so hard for him to leave Sylvia in the first place.

"She's played on it, of course. Whenever the child was sick, she was straight on the phone. 'Ken, can you come over? I wouldn't ask, but he wants to see you.' I can't compete with that sort of thing, Mum. I don't even want to, it's too demeaning.

"It's been in my mind for weeks now. Just to up and leave him. I know he'll try to get me back because really, we are good together, we might have been able to make a go of it, but for Douglas. If he rings, tell him I don't want to speak to him. Whatever happens, I'm not going back. I thought I'd come and work at the college for you. You once said you'd like that. You must be lonely here now, Mum, with Dad gone. We can keep each other company."

She put her hands on the back of

Jasmine's neck and tried to thumb away some of the tension and strain.

"Of course, stay," she said. "We're old enough to share a house and not get in each other's hair."

Jasmine rose and wobbled over to the sink, where she retched quietly over the sound of the running tap.

"You're not—?"

"No, of course I'm not pregnant. What do you take me for? I'm always sick when I'm upset."

"I'll make a cup of tea. Let's take it into the sitting-room. And talk."

She could not identify the mixture of sensation she felt as Jasmine obeyed and followed her into the sitting-room. She had not seen her daughter for some time and now she was shocked by what she saw. Had she never noticed before that almost hungry expression—deprived was the word she was trying to avoid, but really it was the only word for it? She looked like someone permanently on the outside, looking in. Uncertain. Pleading. And at the same time wary, ready to hand out rebuffs before she received them.

Was this what she and Edward had done

to their daughter? *No, not Edward*, said a still, small voice. *You.* Jasmine had surely picked Kenneth Macpherson for the very qualities which now sent him guiltily back to his family—he was a large, soft, kind and receptive man, the sort who would try to untangle wretched emotions and be ready with a clean handkerchief for the mopping-up operations. Although she knew this, she could not stop the next question issuing from her lips.

"Why did you pick him?" she asked Jasmine now, trying not to sound despairing. "You must have known it might turn out like this."

"Why did you pick Dad?"

"I don't know."

"You made me very wretched, the pair of you. I wanted you to be happy together, and you never were."

"Don't hate me, Jasmine. I saw your brother Struan when I was in London, and he hates me. One is enough."

Jasmine gazed at her in shocked amazement. "You saw Struan? And you never told me? Where does he live? Is he married? Is he the slightest bit like me?"

She could not answer for the tears that

284

suddenly choked her. She looked down at her lap, fighting for composure. Impetuously, Jasmine sat down beside her and put an arm round her.

At last she said, "He's a nice, decent person. I'll tell you all I can about him."

How lonely this house had been, with only herself in it! She drew the curtains now, she poured each of them a modest tot of malt whisky Edward had left behind, she threw logs recklessly on to the fire. And she told Jasmine everything she knew about Struan. After a bit, Jasmine unzipped her expensive leather boots and curled her stockinged feet up under her on the sofa and talked about Kenneth. Catherine wondered why she had found it difficult to talk like this to her daughter before. Maybe at the back of her mind had always been the inhibiting memory of her own relationship with her mother, of Lizzie's harsh, judgemental nature. She would not be like this with Jasmine. She was being given another chance. She put out a hand and delicately took a strand of her daughter's hair and tucked it behind her ear.

They had got back to the subject of Struan.

"I shall write to him," said Jasmine. "He isn't getting off the hook, now we've found him. Maybe he'll see me. And maybe I can persuade him to see you again."

"Maybe." She looked at the clock and realized it was getting on the late side to ring the hospital about Colum. Nonetheless she would ring: she would not be able to sleep otherwise. She excused herself and went into the hall.

"Mr. Brodie came through the operation well and is as comfortable as can be expected," said the night sister. "Shall I tell him who called?"

"It is Catherine and tell him I send my love."

Jasmine stood looking at her from the sitting-room door. She hung up the phone and walked towards her, putting her arm round her waist and leading her back towards the fire. What could she teach this uncertain child of hers about living? Only that loving was never simple. Only that it had many guises. Only that, however many times you might walk

286

away from it, it was reborn like the phoenix. And that it was patient and long-suffering as the day.

THE END

This book is published under the
auspices of the
ULVERSCROFT FOUNDATION,
a registered charity, whose primary object is
to assist those who experience difficulty in
reading print of normal size.

In response to approaches from the medical
world, the Foundation is also helping to purchase the latest, most sophisticated medical
equipment desperately needed by major eye
hospitals for the diagnosis and treatment of
eye diseases.

If you would like to know more about the
ULVERSCROFT FOUNDATION,
and how you can help to further its work,
please write for details to:

THE ULVERSCROFT FOUNDATION
The Green, Bradgate Road
Anstey
Leicestershire
England

GUIDE
TO THE COLOUR CODING
OF
ULVERSCROFT BOOKS

Many of our readers have written to us expressing their appreciation for the way in which our colour coding has assisted them in selecting the Ulverscroft books of their choice. To remind everyone of our colour coding— this is as follows:

BLACK COVERS
Mysteries

★

BLUE COVERS
Romances

★

RED COVERS
Adventure Suspense and General Fiction

★

ORANGE COVERS
Westerns

★

GREEN COVERS
Non-Fiction

FICTION TITLES
in the
Ulverscroft Large Print Series

NON-FICTION TITLES
in the
Ulverscroft Large Print Series

We hope this Large Print edition gives you the pleasure and enjoyment we ourselves experienced in its publication.

There are now more than 1,600 titles available in this ULVERSCROFT Large Print Series. Ask to see a Selection at your nearest library.

The Publisher will be delighted to send you, free of charge, upon request a complete and up-to-date list of all titles available.

Ulverscroft Large Print Books Ltd.
The Green, Bradgate Road
Anstey
Leicestershire
England